Foreign Deed

Other Books by Kent Freeland

Norwegian Saga © 2002
Odyssey to Iowa © 2003
Whitney Tales from England © 2006
Journey's Edge © 2007
Prairie Pioneers © 2008
A Street Called Darwin © 2009

Foreign Deed

Kent Freeland

iUniverse, Inc.
Bloomington

Foreign Deed

iUniverse books may be ordered through booksellers or by contacting:

iUniverse
1663 Liberty Drive
Bloomington, IN 47403
www.iuniverse.com
1-800-Authors (1-800-288-4677)

ISBN: 978-1-4620-6325-3 (sc)
ISBN: 978-1-4620-6326-0 (e)

Printed in the United States of America

iUniverse rev. date: 10/21/2011

Preface

✳ ✳ ✳

The idea for this book was initiated by my brother, Alan Freeland. Since he speaks the Norwegian language and has a keen interest in the culture of Norwegian-Americans, he possesses an enormous amount of information on this topic. However, his most valuable contribution was to provide some thoughts that went back to our greatgreatgrandfather who emigrated from Norway and settled in Iowa in the mid-nineteenth century.

Alan helpfully read the manuscript. My wife, Kay, provided a wonderful sounding board as she listened to each of the chapters and offered suggestions.

Foreign Deed is historical fiction, which means that some—but not all—of the events are factual. Some of the information has been altered or fabricated for the sake of producing an interesting narrative.

Chapter 1

✳ ✳ ✳

Otto Arnesen [Iowa 1855]

"I'm not sure I want to be here," thought Otto Arnesen to himself, "but I don't dare tell my wife." It was the year 1855 and Otto and Andrine had made the trip from Norway to the United States with their two children. He had convinced his wife months ago that they should leave their hillside home in Lende, south of Stavanger, and travel over 4,000 miles to the flat land of Iowa.

The railroad car in which they traveled was filled with Norwegian immigrants. The men resembled each other in only two aspects: they were not tall and certainly not overweight. Otto saw a couple of men who wore coats with sleeves that were too long, only the fingers protruded from the opening. In contrast, a few men looked cramped with tight fitting coats. Obviously, most of these men had been given clothes back in Norway by friends who wanted them to have respectable covering on the long trip. The travelers gratefully accepted the clothing, not worried about how well they fit. Otto knew that most of these men were *husmenn*. They had lived in a small rented log houses on land for which they had no claim. A husmann had to work at the farm whenever he was needed, and many of these families lived in poor conditions.

Otto was a *selveier* back in Norway; that is, he had been a farmer who had owned his own land. Sitting on the train now, he felt comparatively fortunate, for he was dressed respectably. His black coat, although common, fit comfortably. Under that, he had a band collar white shirt. Buttoned to the top, it completely encircled his neck. Suspenders held up his wool trousers. His shoes were black with eyelets and laces, made to extend above the ankle. His hands and face were well tanned from his outdoor work. They showed crevassed wrinkles from constant exposure to the sun, wind and rain. Straight brown hair was parted on the left side of his head. It blended evenly into a beard which ran along the edge of his jaw. No moustache though. His blue eyes made a vivid contrast to the rest of his sun-weathered appearance.

His son, Nils, who was seven years old, tugged at his sleeve and drew Otto's attention away from the others on the train. Looking at his son, Otto was reminded why he had left Norway—to provide a better life for his family. The population of Norway had grown tremendously in the nineteenth century, although the amount of livable and arable land could not keep pace. Less than one-fourth of the country was capable of cultivation and nearly all of this was still in forests.

"When will we get to Iowa, *Far*?"

Otto smiled at the boy and replied, "We're already in Iowa, *Min Sønn*. We have been ever since we crossed that big river." The big river was the Mississippi and that was crossed yesterday. They had reached that point by traveling from Stavanger, Norway to New York City. Then they had gone by boats on waterways as far as Chicago, at which point they had joined a group of people who intended to venture westward to the central part of Iowa.

Otto shifted his gaze across to Andrine and to his eight-year-old daughter, Sigrid. "It's for these two children that I decided on this journey to America," he thought to himself. "I can't doubt my choice. Long after I am dead and long after successive generations of my offspring have died, I want my future descendants to remember me for what I gave them— prosperity and security. I have a little bit of money now, but that's not what I want to leave to my children. It's land that I want to leave them. The question now is how to get the land."

Chapter 2

✳ ✳ ✳

Steve Paulson [Iowa 2011]

It was June of 2011. The sandy-haired man put his pencil down and ran through the numbers again. Steve Paulson figured he could buy the land for two million dollars. There were approximately 2,000 acres in Hennepin County, Iowa, that he thought he could purchase for $600 to $1,000 an acre.

"If I tried to buy the land in adjacent counties, it would cost at least ten percent more," he told himself. "I need to buy the farms of some of these local farmers and then I'll have it." Paulson's plan was to obtain a large amount of land and build an entertainment park that would surpass Knott's Berry Farm in southern California and the Six Flags theme parks in various states across the United States; or it might even rival Disney World.

He had been incubating this plan for a year, ever since he had made the trip to the Hennepin County courthouse in Holly Springs to inspect the deeds. He had walked into the county clerk's office last June, up to the second floor, and leaned on the countertop.

"Excuse me, Miss. Could you help me, please?"

A middle aged woman with bottle-blonde hair got up from her desk and came over to Paulson. "What can I do for you?" she replied, laying down a notepad and holding a pencil above it.

"My name is Steve Paulson and I'm interested in looking at the deeds for some land in the county."

"Sure. Who owns the property you're interested in?"

"That's part of my reason for being here. It's farm land, but I don't know the names of all the owners. If I tell you the approximate location, can you show me the appropriate plat maps?"

"Well, we can eventually get that information," said the clerk obligingly, "but I'll first need to access the PIN geocode."

"What's a PIN?" inquired Paulson.

"It stands for Parcel Identification Number, and it gives a piece of property a unique label that identifies it. Each land parcel, from the smallest residential lot to the largest farm has a unique PIN. Farms, in fact, are usually made up of many parcels, each with its own PIN."

"All right," said Paulson with a faint smile. "I'll take your word for that. How do we go about this? How do you find the PINs?"

"Let's look at a plat map of Hennepin County. Follow me." She led the way to an adjacent room containing six tables, along with shelving on all four walls. She walked over to one of the tables on which was displayed a large map of the county, divided into townships, sections, parcels and lots. It also showed all the roads. "Show me where the land is that you want to locate."

Paulson looked for Interstate 37 and the county road which intersected it. "There it is," he said, stabbing the map with his index finger. "The land I'm interested in goes from this gravel road to this gravel road, and then from this gravel road almost to this other one."

"That will probably be a lot of PINs," replied the blonde clerk. "You've identified quite a few farms. Why don't you have a seat at this table and I'll pull one of these books from the shelf."

She plopped a large leather-bound book onto the next table and thumbed a few pages into it. She paused and wrote down a series of numbers and pulled another book off the shelf, writing some more information. She returned to Paulson's table and showed him what she had written.

"I have twenty-eight PINs, representing five owners. I don't know if you're aware of this, but land is divided into townships and each township contains thirty-six sections, six tiers and six columns. A section is square shaped, a mile on each side. It contains 640 acres."

Paulson looked at her and nodded his head. He knew this much about land division.

The blonde clerk took his nod as a signal to continue, although Paulson really wasn't prepared for the elaborate explanation she provided about ten-digit PIN coding, numbering from top to bottom and following an alternating left-to-right, right-to-left reading. Paulson was reluctant to interrupt her lesson on applying PIN numbering to townships, sections and quarter-sections.

Finally he managed to softly interject a request when she made a pause. "Your information has been most enlightening, but it actually hasn't told me who owns the land." Trying not to sound impatient, he gave her a large smile and inquired, "Can you tell me that?"

"Oh, sure. I was coming to that." She wrote down five names on a sheet of paper and held it out for him: Stovdahl, Tesdahl, Sabo, Halvorson and Arneson.

He glanced at the names and then looked up at the clerk. "Are all the farms the same size?"

"A couple are. Do you want the acreage for each?"

"Please," replied Paulson, once again giving her a flattering smile. After a quick figuring, she informed him that Ronald Stovdahl, Milo Tesdahl, and Elmer Sabo each owned 160 acres. Arnold Halvorson and John Arneson each had 320 acres. The sum of all this land was 1,120 acres.

He thanked the Clairol-headed clerk and left the courthouse, thinking that he now had to devise a way to get the land away from those five farmers.

Chapter 3

✳ ✳ ✳

Fort Des Moines (Iowa 1855)

Iowa had become a state in 1846, so not all parts of the state were settled yet. Pioneers had been quick to purchase land in the eastern part, once they had crossed the Mississippi River; thereafter, settlements flowed westward. Railroad tracks had not been completely laid yet in Iowa on the west side of the Mississippi. Moreover, there was no railroad bridge to span the mighty river at Davenport. Therefore, Otto and his family had been forced to travel by wagon after they had ferried from Rock Island to Davenport. After a week and a half of struggling across the Iowa prairie land, they came to a halt on the outskirts of Fort Des Moines.

From the hill where they stopped, they could look down and see a large pocket of civilization, about 2,000 people. Fort Des Moines had originally been established in 1843 as a military outpost, at the junction of the Des Moines and Raccoon Rivers; it was not long after that it became incorporated as a town—in 1852.

"We've arrived in the center of Iowa," Otto told Andrine. "We'll stay here a few days until we decide exactly where we want to go to make our home."

Her husband's words startled Andrine and she turned her head to look at him. Noticing that he was looking straight ahead as he spoke, and not watching her, she finished stuffing a piece of paper into the bottom of the *tine*. She replaced the lid, confident that he hadn't seen her do this. The tine had been her mother's and contained a few items that she considered valuable. The basket looked like a bucket with a lid; but it was made from thin sheets of pine wood which had been steamed, bent and laced together. Wooden pegs had been inserted to strengthen the areas that might receive the greatest wear.

She straightened and moved up closer to him. She brushed away the thoughts that had been stirred by the piece of paper in the tine. "This should be as good a place as any to spend some time, Otto, but where do you think we should find lodgings?"

"Each night on the trail the past few weeks we have slept under our wagon or in a tent," he mused, "but I thought we might seek out a room in Fort Des Moines. I know it will cost us a little bit of money, but it will be convenient when I must visit some of the offices in the town."

They gave their farewells to the others in the wagon party and moved slowly down the sloping land where the city nested between two rivers. The headwaters of the Des Moines River are in Minnesota. It flows southeast for over 500 miles until it empties into the Mississippi River at Keokuk, Iowa. Halfway to its destination it encounters a somewhat smaller river— the Raccoon River, which begins in northern Iowa. To the southwest of Fort Des Moines the Raccoon River curls back on itself and hangs like a droopy lower lip until it moves northeast and joins the Des Moines River. Here, at the junction of these two large rivers, is a piece of land shaped liked an arrowhead, and it points eastward, directly at the Arnesons as they made their way toward it. Fort Des Moines had first been created in 1843 when a company of U.S. soldiers built some barracks at the site. The military presence was intended to protect westward moving settlers from attacks by the Sac and Fox Indians.

Otto pointed to the city, for they had a good view of how the rivers determined the layout of the settlement. "See how most of the buildings are on the west side of the big river? Only a few buildings are on the east side."

"Why is that, Otto?"

"I think it must be that the east side floods very easily, probably lower ground."

They drove their wagon toward the cluster of buildings and Otto reined in at a business with a hitching rail out front. He descended, swatted the dust off his clothes and walked inside. Several customers were scattered around the room, one at the counter buying some supplies. Otto waited until that transaction was completed before he asked his question.

"*God dag.* Good afternoon. My wife and children are looking for a place to stay for several nights. Is there a hotel that you can recommend?"

The clerk was used to all kinds of immigrants traveling through Fort Des Moines, so he wasn't particularly taken aback by Otto's broken English. "You could either stay on this side of the river or the other," responded the clerk.

"Does it matter?" replied Otto.

"It does to some people. You see, we have East Siders and West Siders. The capital of Iowa is being moved from Iowa City to Fort Des Moines, but the exact location hasn't been determined yet. There's a group who believe that it should be built on the west side of the river, but there's another group which feels the new capitol building should be placed on the east side."

"I don't know anything about that," responded Otto. "I just want somewhere that can put up me and my family."

"You can find some places on the West Side. There's the Pennsylvania House, with the price of a meal about ten cents. If you want wheat biscuits with your meal, it costs more. Lodging is twenty-five cents, I believe. You can keep your team of horses there for fifteen cents."

"Is it a clean place?" asked Otto.

"It was a barracks building when the U.S. Army used to garrison soldiers at Fort Des Moines; but don't let its history influence you. It's definitely not a horse stable. It's simple accommodations, but clean."

The clerk continued. "Then there's the City Hotel on Third Street. It was enlarged three years ago. Now it serves several purposes. Besides being a tavern and a hotel, it's the headquarters for the Fink and Walker Stagecoach Company."

"I didn't think there were so many hotels," said Otto, with an air of confusion.

"Oh, yes. And we have more. The Collins House is a first-class hotel. Martin Tucker vowed he would not be outdone in the tavern business. So he purchased an old blacksmith shop at Raccoon Point, reconditioned it and opened it as a first-class house."

Otto did not know how to respond to the array of choices he might make for lodgings, so he said nothing and just stood there.

The clerk sensed that Otto was unable to decide, so he added something else. "If you select a hotel on the West Side, you must be prepared to pay a ferry charge to cross the Des Moines River. Perhaps you would rather stay on the East Side?"

"Yes, that is a fine idea. What hotels are here?"

"If you want the nicest hotel on the east side, try the Demoine House, on the corner of Walnut and First Streets. It was just opened in April. Let me write it down for you." He showed the paper with the name he had just written. "You're probably wondering why it's spelled differently from the name of the town."

Otto was just learning English, so he had not progressed far enough for that fact to cause him any wonder at all.

The clerk proceeded with his explanation anyway. "When the question came up for a name for the hotel, it was decided to call it after the name of the town, but how to spell it was the problem. There was strife between the East and West Side on that, as in everything else. One of our town leaders laid out and platted a town on the East Side and named it Demoine. When questioned as to the spelling, he replied that he didn't care anything about them literary fellows on the West Side; he was going to have it as it was pronounced, and so it remains to this day. The owners of the new hotel adopted the same logic and the hotel was christened with that spelling."

"The Demoine House sounds like it might be too costly for what I'm able to afford. Can you suggest another one?"

"Oh, sure." The clerk told him about a plain place just a few blocks away, the Buckeye Inn. "It looks like a log cabin, which it is. It also houses a tavern."

Otto thought that would be fine. Thanking the clerk, he went outside, told Andrine what he had learned and drove to the Buckeye. After Otto paid in advance at the inn, the owner told him to expect good food: bacon, corn bread and potatoes. "I have one large room on the top floor, said the owner, in which beds are placed along two of the walls. Three men can sleep in a bed, so I imagine that you, your wife and your two children could fit on it. However, the room's pretty crowded because so many men have come to Iowa seeking land. You might want a bit more privacy, so I do have a small room with two beds. You can have one of them, but I'll have to rent the other bed if someone asks for it. There are no wardrobes, so hats, boots and clothes will just have to be shoved under the bed."

They ate their meal at the Buckeye and, since days were long in June, decided they would all go for a walk along the streets in this new town. They paused at one house because they heard beautiful music coming from inside.

"Someone's playing a piano," commented Andrine, who loved music and could sing very well. She began humming. She hummed louder and louder, which attracted the attention of other strollers who were walking by.

"Whose house is this?" inquired Otto of one of the small circle of people who were gathered around him.

"It's owned by Captain West, but his daughter and son-in-law also live there with him and his wife. Captain West bought that piano for his daughter's wedding last year. Her name is Thusa. It was the first piano in Fort Des Moines."

The music in the house finished and Otto urged his family to continue their evening stroll. "Let's go toward the river," he said, with some animation in his voice. "I've never walked along the banks of a river as wide as the Des Moines. The streams back in Norway were narrow."

"Oh, let's do," echoed Nils. "We saw some big rivers here in America, but we weren't able to walk along them."

They reached the river, and picked their way along the edge. Tree roots and bushes made walking difficult. "The sun will be setting soon," said Otto. "We ought to begin our way back to the Buckeye Inn."

Just then they heard a distinct cry from the water. Young Sigrid was the first one to locate the source, which was a man thrashing about in the water. "Help! Help!" he yelled.

"He's right there," shouted Sigrid, pointing to a man just a short distance away.

Seeing that the man was not able to swim, Otto quickly thought how he could help the man. He took off his coat and shoes and bounded into the river. The river bank was slippery and Otto fell backwards as his feet gave way beneath him. He set off swimming toward the flailing man, and soon reached him. He grabbed him by the collar and began to move back to shore. The slick river bottom prevented him from climbing up out of the water. Otto became frightened and wondered how he could possibly get the man up to dry land.

Just then Andrine screamed out to him, "Take hold of the branch, Otto!"

He saw that his wife and his two children were holding out a large tree limb, with the other end just within his grasp. He reached and grabbed it with his free hand. His family started backpedaling and Otto was able to drag the man behind him up onto the grassy shore.

The Arnesons collapsed on the ground beside the man they had just saved. Otto sat up and looked at the gentleman who was coughing and spitting out water from his mouth.

Chapter 4

* * *

One Down [Iowa 2011]

Steve Paulson took the information he had gathered from the Hennepin County courthouse and began to calculate how he could get the property from the five landowners. Arnold Halvorson and John Arneson were neighbors, Halvorson just to the north of Arneson. Each owned 320 acres, so together they owned a section of land. To the south of Arneson's farm were three more farms—each 160 acres—owned by Ronald Stovdahl, Milo Tesdahl and Elmer Sabo. Paulson decided to go after Sabo's first.

Elmer "El" Sabo was a thirty-two-year-old bachelor. While never married, he certainly had lots of women in his life. That was his problem: he never could settle on one because he always found another that seemed a bit better. Then, when he dated that one for awhile, he thought, "Why stay with her, for there must be another one who would be even more desirable." It was this attitude which would soon spell doom for El.

El was dating Lucy Eberhart, who was a librarian at Iowa Community College in Holly Springs. They met this past winter when they were in the waiting room at the local clinic, waiting to get treated for the annual bout of flu. She was reading a magazine when he walked into the clinic waiting room. He sat down so that he was facing her, just a few feet away.

"It seems like I'm here every year at this time," commented El. "How about you?"

She looked up from her *People* magazine and smiled as she answered, "Not really. I don't catch it very often, but this year I skipped my flu shot, and I'm suffering the consequences."

"Flu shot, huh? I don't ever get them. I don't think they really do much good."

Their conversation moved from the problems of winter illnesses to the jobs they had. They exchanged names.

"Listen, Lucy, we'll probably both be feeling much better by the weekend, so would you want to go out for dinner Saturday night?"

"Well, if I'm feeling better, and if you are, too, then that would be fine."

Both recovered from the week's flu and spent Saturday at one of the Chinese restaurants in Holly Springs. They had begun dating and had been with each other every weekend the past four months. This coming Friday night they were going to attend a lecture at the community college on the topic of "Eating Healthy." Lucy was a particular eater, not as much finicky as she was conscientious. She was always careful to watch the calories and grams of fat in the food she ate. The health benefits provided by herbs and food were also on her mind.

El, on the other hand ate what tasted good. He had never watched his diet and paid no attention to the nutritional information on packaged food he bought at the store or took out from the fast food places. He was slightly overweight, but not more than twenty-five pounds. He was often beset by Lucy's questions when they went to a restaurant: "Do you know how many calories are in that sauce? At least 200" or "What do you imagine is the fat gram total in that helping of fried meat? About, fifteen I would think."

He received her comments good naturedly and would sometimes reply with a barb: "I'm a farmer, Lucy, I need all those calories to get me through the day's work." Then he would reassure her that he would start to watch what he ate and change his diet—real soon.

One night he came in from the field and saw a paper sack on his front porch. A typed note was pinned to it.

Hello, El:

Here's some healthy food for you. And I think you will like the taste, too. Tell me what you think of it when we see each other this weekend.

The note was unsigned, but of course he knew it was from Lucy. Inside the sack were half a dozen what appeared to be tantalizing lemon-lime dessert bars. He ate two of them on the spot, licking the crumbs from his fingers. Lucy was right; they did taste good, maybe a little too sweet from an excess of sugar. He'd have to ask her about that when he saw her on Saturday. Today was Thursday. He put the other four on a paper napkin on the counter.

He put the note in the empty paper sack, wadded it up and tossed it in the trash. He gathered up the rest of the paper trash in the rooms and took it out to the fifty-five-gallon barrel, which he used as an incinerator. He lit a match and set the trash afire and then returned to the house. El wasn't ready to eat supper yet, so he decided to eat the rest of the dessert bars.

He began to feel a little dizzy. Perhaps he had worked too hard that day. He took off his clothes and lay down on his bed, thinking that he would eat supper when he awoke. That was the last thing he remembered.

Steve Paulson looked at his watch, which showed ten o'clock. If things were going as planned, Elmer Sabo should be dead by now. He had rented a motel room in Holly Springs on many occasions the past few months and had been able to gather a great deal of information about the five farmers. He knew that Lucy Eberhart was after Elmer to adopt healthier eating habits, so he had mixed up some dessert bars to entice Elmer. The antifreeze he had put in the recipe contained a heavy dose of ethylene glycol. It had a sweet taste, but Paulson figured that would encourage Elmer to eat all of the bars. Ethylene glycol was highly toxic to animals and humans and the special feature was that it didn't leave any trace in the body once it had been assimilated. By the time Sabo was found, an autopsy shouldn't reveal any traces of the poison. It had been easy to drive out to Elmer's farm, walk up to the door and leave the sack where he would certainly see it.

Nobody missed Elmer on Friday. Why should they? He would spend the day working by himself on his farm. Saturday would be the same, until evening came around. When he didn't show up at Lucy's apartment, she called his house. No answer. She drove out and walked into his kitchen. She called his name, but there was no answer. She looked in the rooms and finally found him stretched out on his bed. She ran to the telephone and dialed 911. When they arrived, it was clear that the emergency workers were not needed.

Paulson looked for Elmer's obituary in the newspaper the next week and was satisfied when he read in the *Holly Springs Advocate* "Elmer Sabo died on Friday, June 23 from natural causes. Both visitation and funeral services will be Tuesday at Vincent Funeral Home."

Chapter 5

✳ ✳ ✳

Saving Grace [Fort Des Moines 1855]

All five of the people sat exhausted after the ordeal. Otto pounded the man on the back to help him expel water from his mouth and throat. Nils and Sigrid were capable of nothing more than just staring at the gentleman. Andrine sat on the grass waiting to see if he was going to recover. The man was quite well dressed. He wore a gray suit coat and trousers. He had on a white collared shirt. The black bow tie had come undone and now dangled from his neck. These clothes, along with the shoes he wore, were all soaked.

As soon as the man began to breathe normally, Otto asked him, "Do you think you are going to be all right?"

"I think so. I certainly want to thank you for pulling me from the river. Without doubt you saved me from drowning."

"Can't you swim?" asked Andrine.

"No, I never learned. More's the pity." He took a deep breath before he continued. "I imagine you wonder how it happened that I was in the water?"

Otto and Andrine nodded their heads.

"First of all, my name is Frank Allen, and I'm the Street Commissioner for Fort Des Moines."

Otto raised his eyebrows at this fact, and then introduced himself, his wife and his children.

"I was walking by the river because the Town Council has received a recommendation that a bridge should be built across the Des Moines River. You see, we have no bridges at all at Fort Des Moines."

"I would think that the city needs a bridge," ventured Otto.

"I think so, too. We have a ferry boat; however, that's not adequate. A civil engineer suggested a floating bridge, but there are many ways to construct one. We don't want it to interfere with steamboat, barge and other boat travel on the river. I thought I would come down here along the river and evaluate the situation. I guess I just got too close and slipped on the grass. Down I went. Splash! Right into the river. Before I knew it, I was in over my head. It was lucky that you came along when you did. By the way, what brought you down to the river?"

Otto explained to him that they had come to America and were looking for a place to settle in Iowa. They were staying a few nights in Fort Des Moines until they had decided exactly where in Iowa they wanted to go.

"Where are your lodgings tonight?" asked Allen. He still remained sitting with his legs akimbo, arms resting on his knees.

"At the Buckeye Inn," answered Otto. A blast from a steamboat whistle halted any further conversation. They all turned to look at the ship as the *Valley Lady* wheeled to its starboard and huffed over to the east shore and began docking.

"That's another reason I came to the river this evening. There's a group of us in Fort Des Moines who play in a band. We were invited to Keokuk several weeks ago to perform at a city celebration. We came back directly after playing, but we had to send our instruments back on a separate boat. They're on the *Valley Lady*, so I need to go on board and arrange for transporting them back to my house, or rather my father-in-law's house." He braced himself with his left hand and struggled to his feet.

"Perhaps we should go with you to the boat, for you look a bit unsteady," remarked Otto. "We don't want you to take another bath in the Des Moines River."

"That would be very kind of you," consented Frank.

The five of them made their way to the gangplank and then on board. "There will be quite a few instruments, eleven of them. I just want to make sure that they're all here. Can you wait here for awhile while I do that? I haven't thanked you properly, and I'll do that when I return."

Frank came back announcing that all the instruments were accounted for and that they would be kept on board. The ship would be docked overnight, so he would send a transport worker around early tomorrow morning to bring them to the house.

"What kind of instruments do you have in your band?" inquired Otto.

"Three bugles, a trumpet, two trombones, two French horns, a bass drum, a snare drum and an ophecleide."

Andrine wondered at the unusual sounding word. "What's an ophecleide?"

Frank smiled. "That's the one I play. It's brass and sounds something like a bugle. However, you hold it differently so that the music comes from the horn opening which faces upward. It has lots of keys on it, too. Do either of you play an instrument?"

"I don't, although I do sing; however, Otto plays a fiddle."

"You don't say. We've been looking to add a fiddle to our group. We think that a stringed instrument might blend well with the others. Did you bring your fiddle with you from Norway?"

"Oh, yes, I couldn't leave that behind."

"It's past dusk and you need to be getting back to the Buckeye, but I'd like all four of you to come to our house tomorrow afternoon. It's on Sixth and Walnut, so it's just a few blocks from where you're staying."

Otto looked at Andrine and saw a smile form at the corners of her mouth. "Thank you very much, Mr. Allen," said Otto.

"Please, call me Frank. Anybody who saves my life is entitled to that privilege. We'll see you at two o'clock. Oh, bring your fiddle, too, if that's not too much trouble."

"No bother at all. And we'll be delighted to visit you."

The next morning, which was Friday, Otto decided to visit the United States Land Office. He left Andrine and the children at the Buckeye Inn while he took the ferry across the river. He walked several blocks until he came to a three-story brick building. The first floor was occupied by two banks and a store. The upper floors were the United States Land Office, the River Improvement Company, the Justice of the Peace and several lawyers.

A long line of men extended out of the entry door to the Land Office. His purpose for visiting the Land Office was simply to find out how the process operated: the process of finding available land and then staking a claim to it. This was all new to him. Would there be land he could purchase right here in Polk County? If not, what direction should he go to find open land? When he found land how would he actually mark it so that others would know it had been claimed? Once he marked it, how would he actually find out how much it cost? When he found the cost, how would he pay for it and obtain a deed for the property? So many questions that a new immigrant found puzzling.

He found that the line moved at a snail's pace. After several hours he still was not close to the clerk's counter. He knew he had to be at Frank Allen's house, so he dared not linger longer at the Land Office. Reluctantly, he moved out of the line and began his walk back to the Buckeye Inn.

Otto arrived back at the inn. Andrine and the children were all ready to go. "I've had Nils and Sigrid take a bath, so they're presentable," she said.

Otto had taken a bath when he got up this morning, so he just combed his hair.

"You need something to eat, Otto. I have some bread and cheese and an apple, so you should eat that."

He did so and they left the Buckeye. As they got to the corner of Sixth and Walnut, Andrine remarked to him. "This looks like the same house where we heard the piano music."

"You're right. It is. That was probably his wife playing yesterday."

Otto lifted the heavy knocker on the front door and it was promptly opened by a servant dressed in a black suit. They introduced themselves, were invited into the hall and asked to wait in the sitting room for Mr. Allen.

Frank soon entered and welcomed the Arnesons. Otto remarked how they had been by the house yesterday and had listened to piano music coming from the house.

"Oh, that must have been Thusa. Here, let me show you the piano." He took them into the music room where a beautiful piano stood. "It's a square piano, manufactured by Chickering out of Boston. Before the afternoon is over Thusa will have to play a song for you."

"What are those boxes?" asked Otto. He looked at a number of wooden crates that occupied most of the room.

Frank shook his head and put on a gloomy expression. "There was a mishap with the delivery of the band's instruments. The boxes tumbled off the dolly that was moving them from the steamboat to a wagon. They crashed to the ground and a number of the instruments are damaged."

Just then a woman came into the room and Frank introduced her as his wife, Thusa. She explained that the house really was owned by her father, Captain F.R. West, but that she and Frank lived here until they could find a suitable location to build a house of their own. "Frank has told me all about his rescue. We owe all four of you more than you can imagine."

Two more people entered the room. They were introduced by Thusa as her mother and father. Captain West proclaimed, "Mr. Arneson, I'd like to hear you tell us exactly how the daring feat was accomplished. Frank has already told us, but it's such a remarkable happening, that I would enjoy hearing about it again."

Otto agreed and began to narrate the sequence of events that led to the rescue.

Once the Wests and the Allens had sufficiently praised the Norwegian family, Frank said to Thusa, "My Dear, I told the Arnesons that you would play a song for him on the piano."

She walked over and sat on the piano stool. "Here is one of my favorites. It's 'Jeannie with the Light Brown Hair' by Stephen Foster." At its conclusion, everybody clapped.

"Thusa, Otto plays a violin, but he calls it a fiddle. Would you play a song for us, Otto?"

"Yes, I can do that. If your wife would accompany me, I would like to play the song she just finished." Otto had a remarkable ability to learn a song by hearing it just once or twice. They played a duet which ended with energetic applause.

Frank asked if Andrine and the children would like to go with the two ladies to have some tea and sandwiches in the parlor while Otto accompanied Captain West and himself to the smoking room.

The three men sat in comfortable chairs and began their conversation. "What have you been doing today, Otto?" asked Frank.

Otto explained how he had gone to the Land Office to find out about obtaining land in Iowa. "I'm afraid I was unsuccessful," he said dejectedly. "I didn't get any of my questions answered. In fact, I really don't know if I'm going about this the right way at all."

Frank looked at his father-in-law briefly and then turned his attention to Otto. "I think that I might be able to help you."

Chapter 6

✳ ✳ ✳

Two and Three Down (Iowa 2011)

Steve Paulson felt he could get his next two land owners at the same time. Ronald Stovdahl and Milo Tesdahl had been neighbors for thirty-two years, and they had been at each other's throats for the same length of time. As young boys, they had both attended Holly Elementary School. The school was small, needing only one room for each grade; and, since only three months separated their birth dates, Ronald and Milo had been classmates, confined within four walls, from kindergarten through fifth grade. Confined was the proper term, for the two boys longed for the bells of the day so they could be free of one another—at recess, lunch and at the end of the day.

Their arguments might be over serious differences, but more likely they stemmed from inconsequential matters. On one occasion in third grade Ronald dropped his eraser. Seating was done in alphabetical order, so Milo was directly behind Ronald. Ronald bent over to retrieve the eraser but didn't see it on the floor.

"I bet Milo picked it up," thought Ronald. He looked behind him and saw Milo working on the arithmetic problems assigned by the teacher. "All right, Milo. Give me my eraser," he muttered.

"What eraser? I don't have your smelly old eraser."

"Oh, yes you do." He caught a quick glance toward the front of the room to see if Mrs. McCrotty was looking their way. She wasn't, so he turned again to Milo. "Give me my eraser, Milo. I need to erase some of my arithmetic problems."

Milo shot back, "I bet you do. You're so dumb that you always get the answers wrong."

Ronald grabbed Milo's paper and wadded it up. "Hey!" said Milo. He tried to subdue the fury in his voice. "Give me back my paper."

Mrs. McCrotty's voice from the front of the room halted the boys' altercation. "What's going on with you two?"

"Nothing," both of them answered together.

"If it's nothing, then it can't be very important; so get back to your assignments."

The boys' squabbles were as much a part of their days as brushing their teeth, but without the beneficial results. Milo might knock off Ronald's cap as they entered the school building. As they walked in the hallway, Ronald might come up behind Milo and step on the heel of his shoe, causing Milo to trip. By the time they entered high school, the childhood irritations took on more serious guises. The two boys were big enough so that they could do physical harm to one another.

One spring afternoon during baseball practice Ronald had tossed a ball at Milo when he wasn't looking and hit him squarely between the shoulder blades. Spinning around, Milo saw that Ronald had a smirk that left no doubt as to who had hurled it. Milo stalked over and gave Ronald a hard shove, knocking him to the ground. Ronald sprang up with doubled fists raised shoulder high. Milo moved into his own fighting stance and the two eyed each with true hatred. They circled one another on the outfield grass, throwing occasional punches.

Before the fight got out of hand, Coach Mitchell ran over to break it up. "You boys beat all! You know that? If you spent as much time practicing baseball as you do jawing at one another, you both might be pretty fair players. Who knows what caused your argument this time; but unless you find a way to patch up your differences, I predict that something unfortunate is going to happen to one of you, or both of you, somewhere down the line."

Graduation could not come fast enough for the two combatants, but the evening of the commencement ceremony brought about an incident that outdid any embarrassment created by the antics of either boy in previous years. Practice for the Hennepin County High School commencement was Friday afternoon on May 27. Commencement was scheduled for two days later, Sunday evening. Three hundred tan metal folding chairs had been set up in the gymnasium to accommodate the graduating seniors, the presiding officials, family members and guests. Alphabetical order still prevailed this evening, but the two boys were not seated next to one another for this event. Ronald Stovdahl was to be at the end of the fifth row while Milo Tesdahl's assigned place was on the first chair of row six.

The Saturday before commencement Milo walked to the hardware store and looked over the items he considered buying. After carefully reading the instructions on each of the containers, he made his purchase and went home. The seniors were told to be at the gymnasium thirty minutes before the 7:30 pm ceremony; so when he arrived at 6:15, the gymnasium was empty. Good. That allowed him to do what he needed to do with Ronald's chair.

At 7:30 the high school orchestra began playing "Pomp and Circumstance March." The graduation class marched into the gymnasium, filed into the rows and seated themselves. Milo looked to his right and noticed that Ronald was firmly seated on his metal chair. Wonderful. That's exactly what he wanted. The speakers delivered their comments, and now it was time to acknowledge the graduating class. The Superintendent of Schools asked the first row to rise to come forward. After diplomas were awarded to these individuals, the second, third and fourth rows were called in turn. The fifth row was called and the young men and women got to their feet. Milo watched as Ronald's attempt to rise resulted in a noisy commotion. As Ronald began to rise, the chair came up with him. It banged against the chair next to him and got tangled, causing Ronald to collapse to the floor. He struggled to get back on his feet. Doing so, he tugged at his robe, trying to disengage it from the chair. However, it was firmly attached to the chair. His swiveling only succeeded in banging against his classmates in front, back and to the side of him. Try as he might, Ronald could not disengage himself from the chair. The only thing to do was unzip the robe and let if fall to the floor.

Ronald's frantic performance was observed by everybody in the gymnasium, causing nearly everybody who witnessed the scene to snicker or burst out laughing. Milo led the peals of laughter. He was proud of his success. Milo had brushed on some epoxy glue to the seat of Ronald's chair. The glue was slow drying, but after the elapsed time and Ronald's weight, the glue had the necessary effect. He had become cemented to his chair. What should have been a solemn occurrence became a humiliation for Ronald. The scene of his arch enemy swirling with a chair flying behind him was a memory that Milo would always relish. The only blemish in the picture for Milo was that Ronald would inevitably find out who was responsible for this mortifying prank.

After graduation the two young men remained with their parents, farming the family lands. The Stovdahls and Tesdahls tried their best to reconcile their sons' quarrels, but to no avail. As the years passed by, Milo's father died of a heart attack and his mother moved into town, leaving Milo to operate the farm on his own. Ronald's mother and father bought another farm and let Ronald farm the home place on his own. The two men's arguments spilled over into boundary disputes, animals that got into one another's pastures, and even into women that both men wanted to date. One of their arguments resulted in Ronald coming over to Milo's farm and shooting holes in the tires of Ronald's John Deere tractor.

Steve Paulson had heard the buzz around Holly Springs, Everybody knew about the shooting incident and the consensus was that sooner or later the men would be using their .38 caliber pistols to shoot at each other and not just at their machinery.

Paulson called Milo and asked if he could come to the farm to talk with him about a purchase. Milo said he didn't intend to sell, but would listen to any offer that Paulson might make. Paulson then contacted Ronald and told him that he had talked with Milo and that a meeting had been arranged for later tonight at Milo's house. Would Ronald be able to attend?

"Why do you want me there?" Ronald questioned.

"I'd like to discuss the purchase of both of your properties. And since you're neighbors, I want to make identical offers to the two of you. If you're in the same room together, then there won't be any reason for either one of you to suspect that the other person got a better deal." The explanation satisfied Stovdahl. Paulson hung up the phone and set about the next part of his scheme. He waited until just after dusk, and drove toward Ronald's house, parking his car on the road in the opposite direction that Ronald would take to get to Milo's house. As soon as Ronald's car left the driveway, Paulson pulled his car in and walked to Ronald's house, dialing Milo's number on the cell phone as he walked. Milo answered after three rings.

"Mr. Tesdahl, I thought I'd warn you. I just left Stovdahl's house, for I had gone there to see if he might join us tonight to discuss property sale. He flew off the handle. He has this unfounded notion that the two of us might be trying to swindle him out of his farm. He sputtered that he was going to make sure that didn't happen, even if he had to beat his point into your head with his fists. He'll be at your house soon, I suspect, so watch out for him."

Milo responded just the way that Paulson had expected, with a wild and noisy protest. "If he comes over here expecting me to take a beating, he's in for a surprise. I'll be waiting for him with my little .38 friend. Ronald can choose any of the six bullets in the cylinder if he gets rough with me."

Paulson closed his cell phone and looked for the gun cabinet, which he knew that Stovdahl must have. Inside was the .38 caliber revolver which he picked up, along with a few bullets. Now he had to quickly get over to Tesdahl's house.

Paulson pulled into Milo's driveway just after Ronald had entered the house. Paulson pulled on a pair of rubber gloves and walked through the side door, finding the two men yelling at each other. Milo's gun was lying on a nearby table. Both men turned to look at Paulson and their eyes opened with surprise, for Paulson had a revolver leveled at them.

"What's the meaning of this?" gasped Milo.

"Oh. You mean this revolver?" replied Paulson. "I intend to see if it works."

"Put that away, demanded Ronald," but with a voice that was less of a command than a wish.

"No, I'm going to use it. It's so convenient to have both of you here. The entire community knows how much you two dislike each other. You've fought like Hatfields and McCoys for your entire lives. It won't surprise people very much when they find that you've killed each other tonight."

Paulson pulled the trigger and Milo collapsed to the floor. Keeping the gun aimed at Ronald, he walked over to the table and picked up Milo's revolver. With one shot, using Milo's .38, he dispatched Ronald.

All that was left to do was put the guns in the hands of their lifeless owners. It was a perfect piece to Paulson's plan. He had eliminated two more people who had blocked his way to acquire the land he needed. Now he had to think of a way to dispose of the last two landowners: Arnold Halvorson and John Arneson.

Chapter 7

✳ ✳ ✳

A Helping Hand [Fort Des Moines 1855]

O tto did not understand Frank's offer to help. "How do you mean you might help me?"

"A District Land Office is a busy place," said Captain West. "There are hundreds of men and women who visit it each day. Some even sleep on the steps overnight so they can keep their place in line. Frank and I both know some of the people who run the Land Office and we can talk with them to see if you can get some immediate help. Both of us are friends with Isaac Cooper, who is the Chief Clerk in the Land Office. Frank doesn't know the Register nor the Receiver as well as I; but if he met either one on the street, at least he would be able to have a congenial conversation."

"What are Registers and Receivers?" inquired Otto.

"A Register," explained the captain, "receives applications for entries of land, makes notations of entries on the tract and plat books and prepares monthly reports of all applications for transmission to the U.S. Treasury Department."

Frank now explained the other term. "A Receiver accepts payments for the land, makes and retains in his own office abstracts of entries for which payments are made and sends copies to the Treasury Department."

"It sounds as though these two men do some of the same work," observed Otto.

"There is some overlap, but there needs to be," said Captain West. "Some days the Land Office takes in $25,000 in gold, so there's temptation for theft. The Register and Receiver send information so the Treasury Department can have a check and balance on the figures."

"I plan to call on the Register and Receiver before this afternoon is over," said the captain. "I'll ask if they, or perhaps the Chief Clerk, can give you a private audience to take care of your questions."

"It's important, though," urged Frank, "that you have all of your questions clearly in mind so that you can get your business done as quickly as possible. I'm not sure how much time you'll have alone with the person at the Land Office. Why don't you tell us now what you hope to find out. Perhaps my father-in-law or I know some of the answers."

"The main question I have is where I should go to obtain land so I can begin farming."

"Polk County has little good land left to purchase if you want farmland. My recommendation," advised Frank, "would be to head north. Northern Iowa isn't as settled as central Iowa."

"You know," injected Captain West, "Iowa became a territory in 1838, but the U.S. government began surveying the land before that. There were some settlers who couldn't wait until the land went on sale, so they began planting their claims on a piece of land even before the surveys were completed. These squatters were determined to get a piece of land, although they couldn't buy it until territorial status for Iowa was officially given by the U.S. Congress."

"Were they able to keep their land when Iowa became a territory?" asked Otto.

"In 1841 the U.S. Congress passed the Pre-emption Act, which gave these squatters the first right to purchase up to 160 acres of land at $1.25 an acre. So, the squatter's claim was safe until the day of the land sale, provided he gave ten percent of the money to the Land Office on the day of the sale. Oh, in addition, the squatter had to show proof that a dwelling had been constructed on the land and that he had made improvements to the land."

"If there is land in northern Iowa, how will I be able to pay for it?"

"One way is to pay in a warrant or in scrip issued to a veteran of a U.S. military campaign, but of course you aren't one of those veterans. A second way is to pay cash."

"I have some money with me that I intended to use for land purchase," said Otto.

"If I might ask, how much do you have?"

Otto felt no reluctance to answer the captain's question. "About $300."

"If you want to buy 160 acres, or a quarter section, at $1.25 an acre, then that would be enough, for the cost would be $200."

"How do I know which lands are available for purchase?" asked Otto.

"That's something you'll need to ask someone at the Land Office Monday morning. I don't have the answer for that question. If you'll both excuse me, I need to leave." Captain West departed for his visit to the Land Office, leaving Frank and Otto to return to the ladies and children.

"They're not in here," commented Frank, as they looked inside the music room for Thusa, Andrine and the children. "Wait a minute. I don't see the boxes of instruments, either. I wonder what happened to them?"

He called Thusa's name and heard her reply from another room in the house. The two men walked toward her voice and found the women and children in a back storage room. "I saw that all the boxes of instruments were missing from the music room, Thusa. What's happened to them?"

"Well, it was the most eventful idea that Sigrid had. You wouldn't know that she's only eight years old. We were in the music room after we had refreshments and I was going to play another song for them. Then Sigrid said, "If we didn't have these boxes in here, we could all sit down and listen just like a real audience." Then she asked if she could help move the boxes to another room. That seemed like a good idea, so we fetched the manservant. All of us lifted and pushed and got the boxes to this room. Now they're out of the way until you are able to have them taken care of."

"It sounds as though our guests have been very helpful," beamed Frank. "Your father and I have been active, too. We've made plans to help

Otto get some assistance from the Land Office, but that won't occur until Monday."

"Excuse me while I ask Frank a question," smiled Thusa, as she steered her husband off to the side. The two of them whispered a few things to one another and then walked back to the Arnesons. Frank spoke. "We think it would be a wonderful idea if all four of you could join us for a picnic in the back yard Sunday afternoon. The children can play back there after we eat. I can invite Hiram Gander, who plays a trombone, and Ephraim Goodall, who plays the French horn. If you bring your fiddle, Otto, we can play some songs together. I think the four instruments will sound well as a quartet. I know those two instruments weren't damaged when the boxes fell off the dolly."

Both Andrine and Otto eagerly accepted the invitation. Saturday was spent with the family strolling around the city. They visited the Wests and Allens Sunday afternoon, spending hours eating and playing music. Otto quickly learned Thusa's and Frank's songs and Andrine sang some Norwegian tunes that the men learned to accompany with their instruments. At the end of the afternoon Captain West informed Otto that he should go to the back door of the Land Office at 8:00 Monday morning. Isaac Cooper, the Chief Clerk, would meet him and supply answers to his questions.

Monday morning arrived and Otto walked to the river, where he caught a ferry to the West Side. He went to the back door of the Land Office and knocked, whereupon a short, bald man opened the door. Otto introduced himself.

"Captain West has requested my assistance as you seek a home in Iowa," said Isaac Cooper. "What would you like to know?"

"The most important question I have is where I should go to get land so that I can begin farming."

"It certainly shouldn't be here in Polk County," advised Cooper. "You need to go further north; not as far as the Minnesota Territory, though. You're really removed from civilization if you go to Minnesota, but if you go to Barren County, you'll be close to some towns, supplies and transportation routes."

"How far would that be?"

"Oh, I'd say that traveling by wagon you could be there in four days or so."

"What kind of land is Barren County?"

"Now that's the beauty of the county. You see, it's got plenty of flat land that you could make tillable, and quite a few rivers or streams that would supply you with water. The only drawback is that the county is not heavily wooded, so you'll have to locate a source of lumber to build your cabin and to burn as fuel."

"Has the land been surveyed?" asked Otto.

"That's hard to say. Surveying started in the Iowa Territory back in 1836. By 1850 only about half of Iowa, which had become a state in 1846, had been surveyed. I imagine that some of Barren County is surveyed, but probably not all."

"What do I do if I find land I want, but it hasn't been surveyed?"

"If I were you, I'd find a good natural landmark, such as a sharp bend at a river, maybe a large tree, a rock outcropping, or something like that. Then I'd step off distances from that given point. Approximately 750 paces each way is considered to include 160 acres, more or less. Then I'd drive stakes in the ground at the corners. Write your name on each one. If you had time, you might even plow a furrow connecting the four stakes."

"But how will a Land Office know the exact location of the land I've staked off?"

"We won't. You see, you'll be 'squatting' on it."

"What's squatting?" asked Otto.

"Squatting is assuming ownership of land that really has not been deeded to you. But that's all right if you intend to stay on it. That was provided for in the Pre-ememption Act of 1841. What you need to do to legally establish your intent of ownership is to build a house on it and also break five acres."

Cooper continued. "Then I'd go to the nearest Land Office. One just opened up at Fort Dodge this year, but I suggest you come back here to Fort Des Moines. When you get back to our office, you will fill out an application. The Land Office Register will certify that the land is vacant and available for purchase. You'll then take the certified application to the Receiver and pay him."

"How much will it cost?" wondered Otto.

"The going rate now is $1.25 per acre. You'll get a receipt for the amount. Our Land Office will forward your case file to the headquarters of the General Land Office in Washington, DC, along with a final certificate that declares it eligible for a patent, or deed. Once they do their work in our nation's capital, they will send our office a deed of title for the land. You'll come back to Fort Des Moines and pick up the deed from our office."

Otto asked a few more questions and then thanked Cooper for his assistance. All of this information was exactly what Otto had sought. He returned to the Buckeye Inn ready to tell Andrine that she needed to get ready. They were heading north to Barren County the day after tomorrow.

Chapter 8

✳ ✳ ✳

About Arnold [Iowa 2011]

Arnold Halvorson was a man who represented most people's image of a typical farmer. He was nearing middle age, married, with a family. He was steeped in GM tradition, owning a Chevy Colorado, a versatile pickup truck he could use around the farm, as well as a Buick LeSabre, large enough to accommodate his family of five when they took summer vacations.

Arnold and his wife, Arlene, were devout members of the Calvary Lutheran Church. Their oldest daughter was a freshman at the large state university in Iowa. Their lone son was a sophomore in high school and was hectoring Arnold to buy him a car when he turned sixteen. The youngest daughter was still in elementary school at Holly Springs.

Farming was a strenuous life, causing Arnold and Arlene to have many conversations over the years about whether to stay in the business. "It's Monday morning, but I'd really like to stay in bed awhile longer," Arnold commented to his wife. "The cows can't tell time, but they sure know when it's six o'clock and time for them to be milked."

Arlene sat up in bed and looked over sympathetically at her husband, who was sitting on the edge of the bed. It was five o'clock. Arnold would get dressed and have a quick bowl of cold cereal before he went out to the barn. She would get up and prepare a larger breakfast for Arnold after he finished with the cows. She walked to each of the two children's rooms and rapped on the doors.

"It's almost five-thirty. Chores are waiting," she announced through each of the doors. The kids were good. Each of them knew what to do when it came to feeding the chickens and hogs in the morning. She sighed at the thought of doing all the morning work without their help.

All four of them sat at the kitchen table finishing the eggs, bacon and pancakes that Arlene had prepared. With a "Bye, Mom; bye, Dad," the youngsters left the house to wait for the school bus. Arnold found this was one of the few times of the day when he could catch his breath and have a bit of time to talk with his wife. "Now that Monica has gone to college we have one less helper in the mornings. It makes a difference. In a couple of years Alex will be leaving the house, too, and then we'll have even more to do."

Arlene agreed. "The farm has provided a decent living for us, but we've been lucky that we've not had any catastrophes or major setbacks." Last year we took in about $160,000; offsetting expenses left us with a net of $90,000."

"It's still not enough," said Arnold, folding his hands on the table top. We need to think about a new tractor. That will cost $40,000, so monthly payments will probably be about $2,000. Then the machine shed needs to be redone. Oh, it's about time to reroof our house, too."

"I know where you're going with this conversation, Arnold—Don Mankins at State Farm Insurance."

Lifting both hands in the hair, he uttered, "That's right. He's been after me for two years to work for him as an insurance adjustor. I'd make nearly as much money, but I certainly wouldn't have to work twelve hours a day, twelve months a year."

"But, Arnold, you'd have to travel. You'd be gone one or maybe two days a week."

"O.K. I'll give you that; but that's the only downside." Then the conversation ended as had all the previous ones on this topic—without a decision.

Steve Paulson decided that it would be unwise to have another person killed. One or two deaths within a short period of time in a community could happen, but another one might create some unwanted questions. He decided to work on Arnold Halvorson with another method.

Arlene was glued to the television, watching the weather warnings scroll across the bottom of the screen. The Des Moines television station had placed the annoying, but worrisome, lightning bolt icon in the upper right hand corner of the screen, for upper level winds had blown in from Nebraska. Warm air from the Gulf of Mexico was coming in from the south, which meant that the collision of the two atmospheric fronts were certain to create storms in Iowa. Paulson hatched an idea that would fit in very nicely with the forecast. He only needed to make a few purchases to be ready.

That evening Paulson parked his car in an entry to a field and furtively walked the quarter mile across unplowed fields to the cluster of buildings on Halvorson's farm. The liquid in the container he carried was heavy and made the walk all that more laboring. It was raining heavily, with thunder and lightning shooting savage bolts from the sky. He wondered if this plan was so smart, after all. What if he got struck by lightning? Thank goodness he had bought a plastic container for this job and not a metal one.

He headed for the machine shed and not the barn. Even though he had committed shameful acts the past few weeks, he still had a conscience when it came to some actions; so he did not want to endanger helpless animals. Sliding open the large door, he stepped inside, getting relief from the rain. His clothes were drenched. He shook off as much water as he could and walked to a ladder, propped against the wall. He had intended to throw the gasoline in his container on the walls, but the ladder gave him an idea for a better way to start the fire. He climbed the ladder and stepped onto the rafters. He carefully treaded to the end and then backpedaled, sprinkling gasoline on the large timbers as he moved back to the ladder. Before descending, he threw a match onto the timber and watched it flame up. He noticed that he still had some gasoline in his container, so he tossed that against the wall and flung another match. It was time to make a quick exit.

Running halfway to his car, he turned around to see yellow flames through the windows of the machine shed. What if the rain extinguished the fire, he thought? Even if that happened, the inside and the contents of the building would be ruined. Would that be a loss severe enough to discourage Arnold from staying on the farm? Suddenly a massive blast issued from the machine shed. There was a tractor inside, and once the heat had built up, the gasoline tank exploded. So much for the building being slightly damaged; it was now going to be devastation. Let the authorities try to uncover any evidence that might suggest an unnatural cause for the fire. It would clearly appear that lightning struck the shed, resulting in the detonation.

The following day Paulson basked in his previous night's success, but only for a short time. Now he had to contact Reginald Simpson, his mortgage broker. This was the same international mortgage broker who had been involved in the Trans Syonic oil pipeline two years ago, and that project had been funded to the tune of three billion dollars. Paulson's two million dollars was minor financing, so he was confident that the money would be available when he needed it. Paulson could have selected a mortgage broker who worked with a traditional lending institution, but Simpson didn't ask a lot of questions, such as How do you intend to locate the land you want to buy? or Is the land now vacated? It would be incriminating to explain the procedure by which he planned to acquire the land. All that Paulson wanted was an account established in a reputable United States bank, on which he could write checks to pay for the farms of the people he targeted in Hennepin County. Reginald Simpson called himself a "financial nonfiduciary." In other words, his job was to locate money that might be used for endeavors that had an element of risk or that needed to be shielded from scrutiny.

"When do you think the money will be available to me?" asked Paulson, when he had Simpson on the phone.

"It will be there when you need it. Are you telling me that you're ready to make a purchase tomorrow?" said Simpson, from his New York office.

"Not quite. There's one more property that must come on the market, but that should be soon."

"Very well. Call me when that happens. My lenders can supply your money quickly."

When the conversation ended, Paulson reflected on Simpson's ability to locate sources for the two million dollars. Was it an insurance company, a real estate trust, or perhaps a private individual? No matter. It was a small amount to the broker.

While Paulson gloated in the success of his escapade the previous night, Arnold Halvorson was driving to All Star Realty to arrange for the sale of his farm. Arnold's hands shook on the steering wheel as he recalled last night's unnerving tragedy. Twenty-four hours ago he had wanted to leave the farm, but being driven out by the destruction of the machine shed had made him panic-stricken all morning. He tried to shake off this nervous feeling by concentrating on his upcoming meeting with All Star Realty. How much money would be cleared after they took out their seven percent commission? How quickly would the farm sell? Also, who would the new owner be?

Chapter 9

✳ ✳ ✳

Unexpected Gift [1855]

On Monday, June 25, Otto, Andrine, Sigrid and Nils followed an uneven path out of Des Moines. Yesterday morning they held their worship service, including a special prayer to grant them success on their northward trek.

"When we lived in Lende, we practiced the Lutheran faith," Otto reminded his family. "We congregated at our local church, sang the wonderful hymns and listened to the pastor deliver the message from the Bible. Now we are by ourselves in this land called Iowa, but we must never forget God's word. We must do as the wonderful religious leader, Hans Nielsen Hauge, did back in Norway. We must read the Bible on our own and follow God's instructions as we find them in that book."

The first stop they made was at Ballard's Grove. He talked with Daniel Ballard. "My brother and I made our claims on this piece of land back in 1847. Our father joined us a year later, after we had built our split log houses. Apparently, life on this frontier was too arduous for him, for he died not long after he came here."

"Do you see many travelers come through Ballard's Grove?" asked Otto.

"We've seen a small number the last few years. The frontier has now been pushed from the Mississippi River on to the Missouri. The settlements have mainly been on that east-west line between Rock Island and Council Bluffs. Not many families and individuals have decided to venture into northern Iowa, though."

"Nearly all the settlers who travel north out of Des Moines are just like you. They're looking for cheap land. Ballard's Grove still has a good stand of trees; that's why it's called a grove. I think you'll find that as you go north the trees are found mainly along the creeks and streams. Otherwise, it's tall prairie grass. We have lots of waterways in Iowa. The bulk of them flow southeast."

Andrine listened to her husband continue to talk with the Ballard brothers. In the meantime, she withdrew the piece of paper. How many times had she read it since they left Norway? She wanted to destroy it, but she couldn't. At the same time, she never wanted Otto to find it.

She heard her husband ask Daniel Ballard, "We've been following the Skunk River. How far does it go?"

"You can track it about forty-five more miles to its headwater. If you want to stay with rivers, you'll then need to head east for a short distance and locate the Iowa River, which will flow more or less north, and end up almost twenty miles from the Minnesota Territory."

"We're not certain how far north we intend to go, definitely not to Minnesota."

"This might be a good place for you to stop for the night. My brother and I raise crops and livestock. We provide food and shelter for travelers who pass this way."

Otto decided to stay there for the night. The next morning they were back on the trail within an hour after sunrise. That afternoon they reached the next settlement of Fairview, and Otto and Andrine were delighted to discover that some of the inhabitants were Norwegian. It felt good to converse comfortably in their native language.

"Can we stay the night here, Far?" asked Sigrid and Nils.

"Much as I'd like to, it's too early to spend the night. There are still several hours left today when we can travel," replied their father. Bidding a goodbye and a god dag, the Arnesons climbed into their wagon and set out.

"Wouldn't it be nice if we encountered some people headed our way?" Andrine commented wistfully. "I'd like some company on this long trip."

"You heard what Mr. Ballard said. There aren't all that many who travel to the north out of Des Moines. Most of the settlers stay in the middle of the state."

Daylight was waning and the Arnesons began to search for a good spot to camp. Otto pulled the team of horses to an abrupt halt as he observed a team of horses in the distance hitched to a wagon. "Maybe your wish has come true, Andrine. This appears to be more travelers."

As they got closer, Andrine declared, "This is odd; I don't see anybody." Although the team of horses was startled by the approaching Arnesons, they didn't bolt.

"Look, Andrine, the wagon wheel spokes have been caught in the stump of that fallen tree. That's why the horses didn't gallop away."

Otto walked over to the horses with his arm outstretched. He stroked their necks and patted their shoulders, which seemed to make them more tranquil. He took a few steps from the horses, put his hand to his mouth and issued a loud, "HELLO!" There was no response. He walked over to the wagon and threw back the covering to see what was there. Plenty of cooking utensils, food and other provisions. He yelled once again, getting the same silence as before.

"Where are the people, Father?" asked Nils.

"That's what I'm wondering, Son. The river is next to us, so maybe they've gone to fetch some water. Let's walk a ways to see if we can find them." Otto tied his own horses to the branches of the fallen tree, and the four of them walked toward the Skunk River. When they got to the river, Otto and Sigrid went one direction, while Andrine and Nils went the other. It was decided that each pair would walk about 200 paces and then turn around to meet once again at this spot.

Otto and Sigrid had nearly completed their 200 paces when Nils came running up to them. "Come with me Father," he exclaimed breathlessly.

"What is it? Has something happened to your mother?"

"No." He waggled his head and pulled on his father's arm. "We found somebody. We've got to hurry."

The three of them sped off and quickly arrived at a spot where Andrine was sitting on the ground with a lady's head cradled in her lap.

"The woman is barely alive but I think the man is dead." She pointed to a still body just a few feet from where she sat.

Otto didn't doubt that the man was dead, for he was sprawled on the ground with a large tree limb across his chest. A huge gash was on his head, blood congealed on the wound. The grass was red beneath him, from all the blood that he had lost. A quick check proved that the man had no pulse. He turned to Andrine and the woman. She, too, had several cuts on her head, her left eye was swollen shut and the left side of her head had an unnatural indentation.

"Has she been able to speak?" asked Otto.

"Just a few words. I can't understand what's she's saying. Something about Thomas, who must be her husband. Both of them seem young, probably in their twenties. What do you think we should do?"

"She's still alive, so we need to get her some help. I have no idea what's ahead. The next settlement might not be for another day. But we do know that Fairview is just an hour or so behind us. We need to get them back there."

They got the couple's team of horses disengaged from the tree stump and brought the wagon to the river bank. They loaded the dead man and the unconscious woman into it. Otto said he would drive the other team of horses. Andrine would drive their own team. The children would go with Andrine.

It was after sundown when they made their way back to Fairview. Otto excitedly explained to the Norwegians what they had found and inquired if they had seen the young couple. "Ya," said one of the Norwegians, "they were here this morning, traveling north like you. Their name is Carlson, I think. They said they were going to travel to Minnesota. They didn't know anyone up there, but they intended to start farming."

The man was placed in a shed, with a blanket covering him. A burial was the next event for him. The woman was taken inside a house and attended to by the only person who had any knowledge of medicine, and that was just what he had picked up from practical experience. The woman opened her right eye, seemingly wanting to say something. She was given a sip of water. Andrine asked her, "Please tell us what happened."

"I can't say for sure," she said slowly. "Thomas and I wanted to rest a while, so we left the wagon and lay down under a tree. Oh-h-h!" she moaned, putting her hand to her head. "It hurts so much. Where is Thomas?"

Andrine looked at the others in the group and then back at the woman. "He's resting now. Go on with your story. What is your name?"

"It's Maria Carlson. We heard a loud crack. We were lying in each other's arms. I looked up and saw a big limb falling toward us. I can't see out of my left eye and my head feels like it's being crushed by a boulder. Am I going to die? Where's Thomas?"

One of the Norwegians said, "These kind people found you and your husband and brought you back here to Fairview. Without them, you might have lain there for days."

"Thank you." Maria tried to smile but could not move the muscles to do so.

"Is there any family you need to contact? Anybody at all?" asked Andrine.

"No. We're from Sweden. We have no relatives here nor there. That's why we came to America. All we have is our wagon and the money in our pockets. I want to see Thomas."

Andrine tried to persuade her to rest, but Maria had a premonition that Thomas was already dead and that she was soon to suffer the same fate. "If anything happens to me," Maria said, looking at Andrine, "I want you and your husband to have our horses, wagon and our money. Take what you need to bury us. Can you bury us, please, in the same coffin with our arms resting around each other? That's the way I want to end our lives."

Tears came to the eyes of the half dozen people surrounding Maria. Those were the last words she spoke, for she closed her eyes and slipped out of this world.

"I don't know what to say," mumbled Andrine. "Is it right for us to accept the wagon, horses and money?"

The Norwegian man who had unsuccessfully tried to sustain Maria's life answered, "We all heard her wishes. She and her husband have nobody to give them to. You deserve them more than anybody else."

Andrine leaned over and kissed Maria on the forehead. "Thank you," she whispered.

One of the Norwegians cleared his throat and asked, "You already have a wagon with a team of horses. I've been saving up to buy one. Now if you agree, I'd like to purchase the Carlson's wagon and horses. I'll give you $150 for it."

Otto knew what he paid for his own wagon and horses, so he felt that $150 was a fair price. "That will be acceptable to me."

As they left Fairview once again the next morning, Otto reflected on what had transpired the past twenty-four hours. "It's amazing, Andrine. We had nearly $300 yesterday. You might say we inherited supplies, horses and a wagon. Not only did we sell the horses and wagon, but we also sold some of the supplies; plus we were given gold coins. Now we have about $700. I feel like a king with all this money."

"You're right, Otto. It seems almost too good to be true."

The delighted couple hugged one another over their unexpected good fortune.

Chapter 10

* * *

Closing In (Iowa 2011)

Steve Paulson was ready now to make his move on the available land formerly owned by Sabo, Tesdahl and Stovdahl. John Arneson still owned his 320 acres, but Paulson needed to purchase the other lands before anybody else decided to acquire them. Sabo had been a bachelor, and had died intestate, meaning that the state of Iowa would in effect dispose of his property. The Prairie Citizens Bank held the mortgage and would offer it for sale.

Both Stovdahl and Tesdahl owned their farms, with no outstanding mortgages. Tesdahl, like Sabo, had been a bachelor, so his 160 acres would most likely be up for auction. Stovdahl's only surviving sibling was a sister who had never taken an interest in running the farm. In fact, she had moved to another state, so Paulson assumed that the farm would be up for sale soon.

A phone call to Reginald Simpson resulted in $150,000 being transferred to an account at the State Home Bank in Des Moines. This would be enough to cover the earnest money required when he tendered his offer to buy the three farms.

Paulson parked his car in the lot intended for customers at Prairie

Citizens Bank and walked inside. "The interior is tastefully done," remarked Paulson to himself as he surveyed the dark wood ensconcing each of the four cashiers. Three glassed offices were aligned against one wall and a hallway led to other offices in the anterior of the building. He walked across the tiled floor to the receptionist.

"My name is Steve Paulson. I'd like to see Mr. Aldershot."

"He's with somebody right now, but will probably be available in about twenty minutes," she said with a white-toothed smile.

"That'll be fine. I'll just wait."

Paulson walked over to a wing back chair and sat down. He rehearsed in his mind what he would say to the loan officer, all of it to be a bald-faced lie.

Within fifteen minutes the receptionist announced, "Mr. Aldershot will see you now." She led him to one of the glassed offices and went back to her desk.

At the same time he extended his hand, he stated, "My name is Steve Paulson."

"Good to meet you. I'm Greg Aldershot."

After a few comments on the weather and the nice appearance of the bank, Paulson got directly to his reason for the visit. "I'm looking for a farm where I can live part time. I'll stay in Des Moines most of the time."

"What do you do in Des Moines?"

"Investments primarily. I have clients who ask me to manage their money, either by recommending stocks or bonds or by suggesting business opportunities where they can supply needed financial backing."

"Why did you select Hennepin County?"

"I travel to the Twin Cities frequently and have gotten off the interstate many times to investigate possible sites. I like Hennepin County. It's attractive and the land is moderately priced."

"Do you have any particular land in mind, Mr. Paulson?"

"Yes. I understand that Mr. Elmer Sabo died recently and that his farm is up for sale by your bank. I'd like to purchase his land."

"Very unfortunate about Elmer. Sort of a strange death. He hadn't been ill, just the flu." Aldershot paused a minute before finishing. "Apparently his heart just stopped functioning. But, yes, his farm is for sale. We'll probably auction it unless you want to make an offer at the price we have established."

"And what would that be?"

"The bank is asking $100,000."

"I'm definitely interested. How much would you need for me to place down to initiate the purchase?"

"Ten percent would do."

"All right. Do you want to begin the paper work today?"

"That won't be possible, for we need to draw up the documents. We could have them ready the day after tomorrow. Would that be acceptable?"

"Sure. Wednesday will be fine with me."

Paulson left the bank content with knowing he would be back in forty-eight hours to claim one piece of his dream. He felt that on that same day he might also be able to obtain the second piece, for Milo Tesdahl's farm was going to be auctioned.

On Wednesday morning, a man parked along the road and walked a few hundred feet toward the crowd which had gathered on the farm yard. He pulled the cap tighter down onto his dark hair. Normally the cap would have been too large, but today it was a good fit. It had to be a bit oversize to encompass the wig he had bought. None of his sandy hair protruded beneath the hairpiece. A pair of dark-rimmed glasses completed Paulson's disguise.

He approached the table where bid numbers were being issued for the auction of Tesdahl's farm. He was given a card with the number "17" printed on it. "Good," he mused, "the low number means that there should be few bidders."

He had barely moved into the back line of the crowd when a short, heavy-set man climbed on a table and began the auction. "We're auctioning 160 acres of farmland, with buildings, no farm equipment. Purchasers will sign a contract agreeing to pay ten percent down today and the balance in full at closing. Purchaser will assume all taxes prorated effective with the purchase date. Now let's begin. Do I hear thirty thousand? Yup!" He pointed to a man with a hand raised at the front of the crowd. "Got thirty. Do I hear thirty-five?"

The auctioneer's voice rang loud and rapidly. Fifteen minutes later only two people were still bidding. Paulson had the last bid at seventy thousand dollars. The competitor shook his head from side to side. That was it. Paulson now owned the Tesdahl farm.

That afternoon, after he had removed his disguise, he visited the Prairie Citizens Bank and completed the arrangements for the purchase of Elmer Sabo's 160 acres. He now had 320 of the 1,120 acres He would double that when he visited All Star Realty tomorrow and make an offer to buy Arnold Halvorson's land.

The next day, which was Thursday, he sat across the desk from the All Star real estate agent. "I don't think I can pay the $160,000 asking price for the Halvorson farm," commented Paulson, as he tapped his pen on the desk.

"The farm is worth every dollar of that, Mr. Paulson."

"Perhaps, but I can only offer $130,000."

The agent drew back his head and stated, "I very much doubt if Mr. Halvorson will accept anything less than $160,000. He is sure to have lots of offers and he'll just wait until the right one comes along."

Paulson silently thought, "That won't happen. Halvorson wants to get out from under that farm and will take the first offer that comes close to his asking price." Instead, Paulson smoothly commented to the agent, "Please contact Mr. Halvorson and see what he thinks of my proposal. I'll call you back this afternoon."

When Paulson called back, the agent said Halvorson wouldn't accept $130,000 and wanted to know how much higher he could go. The last comment alerted Paulson to the fact that Halvorson would jump at the chance to take whatever counteroffer might be made.

"I'm prepared to give him $140,000. I'll step outside while you call him to see what he says."

Paulson didn't have long to wait, for the agent opened the door after a brief phone conversation and said that Halvorson accepted, resulting in Paulson having well over half of the acres.

Chapter 11

✳ ✳ ✳

Arriving in Northern Iowa [1855]

The Arneson family knocked along the grassy terrain, heading northeast to the Iowa River. Otto always drove. Sometimes Andrine would sit beside him and the children walked; or sometimes all three would be in the back of the wagon. At this time, though, Sigrid was sitting beside her father while Nils was walking alongside the wagon. Alone in the back, Andrine had opened the tine once again, pulling out the letter to reread it. She knew it by heart and was a bit ashamed that she could not make herself destroy it. But the words written by Casper years ago reminded her of the little boy they had brought into the world. He had been given away before a name could be selected. Who was to blame for that? No one knew about the baby, for she had carried the child without showing any signs of pregnancy to her friends and family. Unfortunately, Casper could not marry her. She couldn't keep the baby by herself. How old would he be now? Ten years old, two years older than Sigrid. She had never heard from Casper, only the letter which had arrived just before Otto and she had left for America. In the letter, he had explained that he couldn't bear to lose the infant son, so he was going to try to find him. Andrine felt as though she was less of a person than

Casper, for he was going to attempt to recover the boy, whereas Andrine had abandoned him.

Nils's loud shouts brought her thoughts back to the Iowa prairie and she replaced the letter at the bottom of her tine. "There's a river ahead, Far," yelled the boy.

"It's not the Iowa River, Nils. Not the one we want. The men back at Ballard's Grove said there would be a couple of creeks before the Iowa."

A number of small log homes and some other buildings were arranged along the banks of the creek.

"I see some men and women working the gardens and fields around the houses," said Otto to his son, "but I don't see any children. I wonder why not?"

Otto flicked the reins on the horses' rumps and the animals moved out toward the nearest group of men, who stopped their work.

"Hello, traveler," said one of the men as he removed his wide-brimmed straw hat and wiped his brow.

"Good day to you," responded Otto. "I'm headed for the Iowa River. Would it be far?"

He introduced himself as William Dobbins and then responded with, "Only five miles to the northeast. This is Honey Creek, so the next river is the one you want. A group of us came here from North Carolina three years ago and started this settlement."

"I find it strange that there are no children around," Otto said.

"Oh, there are lots of children, but they're in school. The building over there," Dobbins pointed with his left hand, "is our schoolhouse. We're Quakers and we call ourselves the Honey Creek Settlement. Our meeting house stands next to the schoolhouse. What is your purpose in coming to this part of Iowa?"

Otto explained that he had come from Norway and was seeking land.

"It seems to me that you should be able to get that along the Iowa River. The only town of any size where you're headed is Eldora. It was developed about three years ago, and now has probably over 200 inhabitants."

The Quakers invited Otto to stay with them at Honey Creek that night, because that would allow them to reach the Iowa River tomorrow in daylight hours.

That last week of June Otto did what Isaac Cooper, the Chief Clerk at the Des Moines Land Office, had advised. The Norwegian immigrant started from a natural point on the Iowa River, which was where it made a nearly ninety-degree turn alongside a copse of trees. With each measured step he took on the U.S. government land, he became more filled with the pride of ownership. He drove the last of the four corner stakes into the ground, took off his hat and wiped his sweaty brow.

"There!" he exclaimed, "The land is mine!" Otto looked around at the 160 acres of the southeast quarter of section thirty-four, on which he had just staked a claim.

Otto wasted no time erecting a shanty in which the family lived until a more comfortable house could be built. When living in the shanty, Andrine tried not to grumble. However, some things deserved complaining. One morning Andrine wakened when daylight was just filtering in through the cracks in the shanty.

"Wake up, Otto! What is that?" A black and white creature was moving around not more than five feet from where the family slept.

Otto had seen these animals before, but never had been this close. "Don't move," he whispered, for he did not want to waken the children. "That's a skunk." Two more of these animals, smaller than the first, had joined the mother skunk.

"Just treat them kindly and don't move around. If they get agitated, they might spray a most terrible stream at us. It smells awful and will last a long time."

After five minutes of wandering around in the shanty, the skunks lost interest and waddled back outside.

"I've endured the howling of wolves, the screeching of owls and even snakes in our shanty, but honestly, Otto, I just can't take any more of this. We can't keep living in this shanty. I can't even cook in here because we might burn it down."

"You're absolutely right, Andrine. Why, this shanty doesn't even have a door. I just prop up some logs I've bound together. The roof is only made from elm bark, and now that's curling up because it's dried out. We've been in this shanty for two weeks. As sure as I'm standing here, I'll start building a cabin next week."

True to his word, Otto began to plan for the family's cabin the next morning. A grassy area seemed to be the best site, for it wouldn't demand the hard work of removing trees. His thinking was interrupted by the sound of Nils, running from the river. "Far! Far! Look what I found!" He extended his closed fist to his father and opened it, revealing some yellowish-looking flakes.

"Where did you find these, Nils?"

"I was playing down by the river and saw them in the water."

Otto knew about gold, for he had heard about prospectors who had rushed to California just seven years earlier, searching for riches. Could this be a find like the one in California? Might he be able to pan for gold and acquire a fortune right here in Iowa?

"Show me where you found these, Min Sønn."

The two made their way to the banks of the river. "It was right there by the fallen tree, Father." Staring into the water, he could not see anything which resembled the flakes that Nils had discovered. Maybe the gold was farther upriver, and these few flakes had washed down.

Deciding to return tomorrow for a closer look in the river, Otto made his way back to the shanty, Nils following by his side.

Otto had two things on his agenda: build the cabin and investigate the river for gold. Although his intentions were true, he never had to deliver on them, because that afternoon a neighbor came by to introduce himself. His name was Egil Larson and he was also from Norway.

"I'll admit to you I settled here for only one reason," Egil told Otto, "and that was to find gold."

Otto's mind came to full alert when he heard Egil Larson mention "gold." "Is there really gold around here?" he asked with genuine interest.

"People used to believe that. About three years ago a man named John Ellsworth claimed to have found gold along the shoals of the Iowa River," related Egil. "That caused a lot of men to move in, hoping to get rich. Nothing really developed from that. It turned out that there was just a very small amount of gold that was discovered."

"My son found some yellow flakes this morning. I think they might be gold. Would you recognize it?"

"I sure would. Where is it?"

Otto asked Egil to follow him to the wagon, where he withdrew a bucket, lifted the lid and took out a folded piece of paper. Inside were the golden flakes. Egil looked closely at them and then took out his knife, pushing down on the flakes. "No, this isn't gold. They're too hard. If this were real gold, I could smash them with the tip of my knife. This is pyrite, which is called 'fool's gold.'"

Otto's hopes were dashed. His thoughts of riches flew away with the words of Egil. "What about your prospecting? Did you find any gold?"

Egil wagged his head. "I bought my miner's pan and a shovel, but all I found was a bit of dust—the size of a pinhead. Imagine, working in that river for months and only getting out about twenty-five cents worth! The only thing I have to show for my years here is bent fingers from the hard work," Egil scoffed. I just want to get out of this place. When I came to Iowa I had traveled through St. Louis. Now I intend to go back to St. Louis and find a new life."

"What are you going to do with your land?" asked Otto.

"Who knows? If I can sell it, fine; but if not, then I'll just leave it and run away from it."

"How many acres do you have?"

"Eighty," responded Egil. "Do you want to buy it?"

"Ya, if you are willing to sell it cheaply."

"Give me twenty dollars and I'll give you the deed."

Otto made a quick decision. He was going to buy his 160 acres for $1.25 an acre. He could get Egil Larson's for just one-fifth of that. He would be a fool to pass it up. "Do you have any buildings on the land?"

I have a cabin and a shed. The shed is small, just big enough for a horse and a cow and some tools.

"A cabin," Otto thought. "Andrine can have her cabin immediately."

"Ya, I'll do it. I'll buy your land."

Chapter 12

✳ ✳ ✳

Last One [Iowa 2011]

John Arneson farmed 320 acres of land with the help of a neighboring farmer. He had intended to retire shortly after the tragedy which struck two years ago. His daughter, who lived in Wisconsin, visited him and his wife at that time. Their only child, Emma, was a sales representative for a pharmaceutical company. She enjoyed a fast-paced life in Milwaukee and had never married. On this visit, she invited her mother to accompany her on a shopping trip to Des Moines.

"Let's go for the weekend, Mom. My treat. We'll stay at the Farragut Hotel downtown, attend a performance of the symphony, and then do some shopping."

"Oh, that sounds like fun, Emma, but I don't know. I'm giving a program at the homemaker's club Tuesday evening."

"No problem. We'll leave on Friday morning. That will give us a long weekend in the city. We'll be back here at the farm Monday night."

The mother and daughter were entirely opposite. Emma was impetuous and had energy to burn. Ruth, on the other hand, always considered things carefully and was slow in making decisions.

"What if there aren't any tickets left for the symphony?" asked Ruth.

"So what if there aren't? We'll just go see a movie then. No more objections. We'll look for a new winter coat for you in Younkers and a pair of shoes to go with it."

With one last reservation, Ruth said, "Let me ask your father. He might have some other plans for us this weekend."

Knowing that her mother always had to check with John before she left for even a couple of hours, Emma replied, "That's fine. He'll tell you the same thing he told me when I told him about my brainstorm this morning. He'll encourage you to go."

On Friday morning mother and daughter entered the gravel road on their way to Des Moines. Emma hated the gravel roads, for the dust swirled behind her and left a coating on her new Ford Mustang. She crawled along until she arrived at the entrance ramp for I-37. Now she could make up for the snail's pace she had endured on the gravel road. She pushed the pedal to the floor and the car accelerated to seventy miles per hour.

"Please slow down, Emma. I just hate it when you drive so recklessly. Her daughter looked over at her mother and smiled. "This isn't fast, Mom The speedometer goes all the way up to 120, you know."

The Mustang shot up to eighty and approached a ridge. The crest was just high enough to prevent Emma from seeing that a car in front of her had pulled into the passing lane to maneuver around a very slow-moving truck. By the time she saw the danger, she had no choice but to steer into the ditch on the right in order to avoid the vehicles which occupied both lanes in front of her.

Once in the ditch, the Mustang rolled several times and smashed into the concrete bridge railings. It came to rest in a small stream, upside down, with all four tires spinning. Both mother and daughter were dead from the impact. John Arneson lost his two prized loves and seemed to lose his desire to keep on living. He thought that maybe by continuing to operate the farm, he could go on; but that wasn't the case. He discovered that the house reminded him too much of the wonderful times he had shared with Ruth and Emma. Farming became a drudgery. The recent deaths of his neighbors, Elmer Sabo, Ronald Stovdahl and Milo Tesdahl, deepened his despondency. Furthermore, Arnold Halvorson's move stirred him to consider selling his own farm and move away—maybe to Holly Springs or to Council Bluffs, where one of his cousins lived.

Steve Paulson sat in his hotel room in a city south of Holly Springs. "It would be too risky," he decided, "if I attempt to eliminate John Arneson. People in the county might become suspicious if another person met an untimely death. I think I'll contact Reginald Simpson to see if he can think of another way to acquire Arneson's farm.

"I believe I have a way to carry this out, Steve," said Simpson, when Paulson telephoned him. "It would be unwise if you were to buy Arneson's farm so soon after acquiring the other property."

"But that's an essential piece of the tract of land that I need to implement my plan," complained Paulson. "He's selling it now."

"Let me finish," the financial agent continued. "Your name will never be connected to the purchase of Arneson's land. I'm associated with a real estate company. I'll have one of my representatives fly to Iowa and visit All Star Realty, making an offer for the 320 acres."

"Won't All Star want to know what you intend to do with the farm? I'm concerned that All Star will want to know why another real estate company is buying the land."

"There's nothing extraordinary about that," reassured Simpson. "It's entirely plausible if a real estate company purchases land with the intent to develop it or to hold it for speculation, or even to buy it for another party."

Paulson was relieved to hear this. "Fine. Then I can later buy it from you, right?"

"That's the way it works," said Simpson. "You might as well disappear from Hennepin County for awhile until the transaction is completed. I'll let you know when the deal is finished."

Everything went as Simpson had predicted and within two weeks Paulson was the owner of 1,120 acres of farm land. His thoughts now turned to how he would go about contacting the Iowa Department of Transportation so that the county roads could be truncated, which would enable the five farms to be joined together for the vast entertainment park. Signs would have to be erected on I-37, too, directing traffic to the park. Creating and copyrighting a theme park logo, advertising for the theme park, merchandising items for the theme park, constructing infrastructure for the park facilities, hiring theme park staff. So many things to think about. However, these would come later. First would be the elimination of the gravel roads. He needed to have an uninterrupted expanse of land so that he could have surveyors and construction contractors begin their work.

Chapter 13

✳ ✳ ✳

Making a Home [1855]

Otto was looking forward to the fall. His family had moved into the cabin vacated by Egil Larson. The shed was large enough to contain the horse with room left over for a cow that he wanted to buy. Probably the best way to obtain that would be to make a visit to his neighbors, whom he hadn't met yet, to see if they had one to sell. He had made several forays upriver during the last few weeks hoping to stumble on some more of the yellow flakes, maybe even proving Egil Larson wrong when he had stated that the only mineral that could be found would be fool's gold.

On one of those treks he had noticed a wisp of smoke in the distance. There were almost no trees at this stage of the Iowa River, so it was easy to see the smoke drifting toward the blue sky. Someone in the house no doubt was doing cooking over a stove. Otto approached the cabin, a dog barking in front, and knocked on the door. A voice from inside could be heard: "Ya, don't go away. I'll open the door.'"

When the door opened, Otto thought he was looking at his twin, for the man was his height, straight brown hair, parted on the left. He had a narrow beard that traced the edge of his jaw. Blue eyes completed the match. When the man spoke, Otto knew that he was speaking to a fellow Norwegian.

"God dag. Hvordan står det til?"

Otto couldn't believe it. He stood there for a moment listening to the man's greeting: "Good day. How are you?"

Then Otto replied with his own, "Bare bra, takk." Fine, thank you.

The accent of the man was as familiar to Otto as though he were back in his home village of Lende. "You are from southern Norway, isn't that correct?" inquired Otto.

"Ya, just south of Stavanger." This generated an animated conversation between the two, from which Otto learned that the man was Sigurd Helland and he was living here alone.

"I came over by myself because there wasn't money enough to pay the passage for my wife and two children. I've been here for two years now and I have arranged with a transportation agent in Norway for the rest of my family to sail to America. I paid $18 for the ship passage for my wife from Stavanger to New York, then $50 more by railroad to Chicago. The two children's fares were half that. Once they get to Chicago, they'll need to buy additional fares to get to Dubuque, Iowa and then on to Eldora. I've told the storeowners to expect them, so once at Eldora, my wife can ask someone to ride out to tell me they're here. Then I can ride into the town and pick them up. I'll be so happy to see them! They'll be here sometime in September, I hope."

Sigurd told him that three other neighbors were Norwegians from the *fylke*, or county, of Rogaland. "There used to be another Norwegian who lived nearby, Egil Larson, but I believe he left for St. Louis."

"That's right," said Otto. I bought his eighty acres from him. That's next to the 160 acres which I laid claim to earlier this summer."

"Have you actually purchased the land?" inquired Sigurd.

"Yes, I have the deed for Larson's property, but I haven't a deed for the land I staked out."

Helland expressed some surprise. "Oh, you need to do that as soon as you can, for sometimes unscrupulous men try to steal a claim. You should travel to the U.S. Land Office in Fort Dodge or Fort Des Moines and get a deed."

Otto thought of Isaac Cooper, the Chief Clerk of the Fort Des Moines Land Office, who had also told him to do this very thing. "You're exactly right. I must make plans to travel to Fort Des Moines."

With a wag of his head, Helland said, "It isn't easy for us emigrants to know everything about acquiring land. Moving to a new country, I've found that learning a new language isn't the only problem I've encountered."

"What kind of problems are you speaking of?" wondered Otto.

"Like I've said, there are all these officials that have to be visited before one of us can actually say that we own a piece of land. Another one is getting food. I can certainly grow some crops, but I can't eat raw grain. I had to find a mill where I can take the grain so it can be ground into flour."

Otto hadn't thought about that, for he hadn't planted fields of wheat or corn yet. He wouldn't do that until next spring."

"Then there's the money," Sigurd continued. "There's so much of it. I don't mean that everybody is rich. I'm certainly not. What I mean is that there are so many different kinds of coins and paper bills."

What Helland hadn't realized was that in 1855 the United States had no national currency. Coins were privately minted. More than 1,000 chartered state banks and corporations churned out a dizzying stream of colorful bits of paper, resulting in over 10,000 different kinds of notes being passed around in the country.

"See now. Here's what I mean." Sigurd reached into his pocket and pulled out a blue and white bill with a denomination of one dollar. "I got this from a bank when I was in Fort Des Moines. It has a picture of a woman standing beside a cow. I tried to buy something at a store in Eldora, but they said they wouldn't take it. 'Go back to Fort Des Moines,' the shopkeeper said. 'Spend it there.'"

Otto reached into his own pocket to see what one of his notes looked like. "Mine has a ship."

"That one's probably all right," reassured Sigurd. "Storeowners in Eldora will most likely take that one. However, they might not give you a dollar in goods for it. Maybe something less. Now, you've got to keep in mind that it could be counterfeit, too. That's a whole other problem."

"I had no idea that money was so undependable," cried Otto.

"Oh, yes, you know what they say back in Norway: 'When it rains on the pastor, it drips on the choir.' In America, if a problem affects a particular state, then all the other states will experience it, too."

"What can a person do, then, about this money problem?" posed Otto.

Sigurd wasted no time in answering. "Don't trust the banks. Get gold and silver coins. Don't leave your money in any bank. Keep it at home, where it will be safe."

Otto was also quick with his rejoinder. "It seems to me that having land is a wise thing to do with your money. After all, God isn't making any more land. It can only get more valuable."

The conversation reinforced Otto's dream to obtain as much land as he could and pass it along to his children. It appeared that Sigurd might have a similar inclination. He had to meet these other three Norwegian neighbors, for he had this odd mental flash about the five of them banding together in order to protect their property and safeguard whatever assets they might accumulate during their lifetimes. He had no idea of how they could join with each other, nor even what exactly they could accomplish. However, he just felt that a group of Norwegian immigrants would benefit if they looked out for their own interests. After all, many small brooks make a big river.

As Otto prepared to return to his cabin, Sigurd said, "Every Sunday we four Norwegian families meet to worship. Please join us."

Otto had missed the companionship generated by attending a worship service. It had been months since he and his family had done so back in Norway. "I'd like that very much, Sigurd. Where do you meet?"

"Per Bremse has a rather small cabin," replied Sigurd, "but Jacob Anderson and Torin Halvorson have houses, so we alternate our meetings in the two large places. This Sunday it will be at Torin's. If you bring your family to my place, I'll show you the way."

"Takk, thank you. Do you worship the Lutheran way?" inquired Otto.

"Of course. We all have a deep affection for the faith of the Lutheran Church. Since we're all farmers, and being common people, we also practice the worship principles established by Han Nielsen Hauge."

"What a great man he was," praised Otto. "Did you ever see him back in Norway?"

"Oh, no. He died before I was born. But my father saw Hans Nielsen Hauge when the preacher was traveling around the country. I recall my father saying that the man spoke like he was on fire, moving his hands up and down and hopping from one foot to the other. He had a prominent jaw and it jutted out farther than normal when he wanted to emphasize a point. None of us men have a personality like Hauge, but we do try to follow his practical outlook on religion."

"That's good to hear," said Otto. "My family and I will be here at your cabin Sunday morning."

On the next Sabbath Otto, Andrine and the two children rode up in their wagon and Otto introduced them to Sigurd Helland. Sigurd saddled his horse and led the way to Torin Halvorson's house, which was a log cabin with several rooms on the ground floor: a kitchen and eating area, a large living area and a bedroom. A loft was built along one of the walls in which the four Halvorson children slept. Twenty-four people were crammed into the cabin: Otto's family; Sigurd Helland; Jacob and Kari Anderson and their five children; Per and Berta Bremse and their three children; and Torin and Jakobina Halvorson with their five children.

This is the kind of act which had gotten Hans Nielsen Hauge in trouble in Norway and thrown in jail in Norway, for itinerant preaching and religious gatherings held without the supervision of a pastor were not accepted in that Scandinavian country. It was different here in America. This group of twenty-four people did not need a trained pastor to lead them to salvation. They could find the way on their own. They sang some hymns from *Thomas Kingo's Hymnbook*, such as "On My Heart Imprint Thine Image" and Martin Luther's old standby, "The Church's One Foundation," familiar to the adults and children alike. Berta Anderson accompanied the voices by playing her psalmodikon. Otto was impressed with how she was able to coax sweet music by running a bow over the single string on the wooden instrument.

After the singing, Per Bremse opened his Bible and read Revelation 3:20. "Behold, I stand at the door and knock. If any man hear my voice and open the door I will come into him; and I will sup with him and he with me." Bremse spent a few minutes explaining his view on these words. "Prayer is not a complex activity. It doesn't result for me only after a lengthy and difficult time of thought. It does not happen for me only after I have spent days agonizing over the matter. Prayer happens simply by me being willing to open the door to Jesus Christ." Each of the men and women in the room then offered their own solemn prayers inviting Jesus to come into their lives.

Throughout the service Otto looked around at the group. Were they all like Sigurd Helland: diligent and industrious? It was important that they had these characteristics which Sigurd possessed if he was going to approach them with his idea. Sigurd had told him, "Otto, if you present your plan to the men, I will solidly vouch for it and support you."

Chapter 14

* * *

Disappointment [Iowa 2011]

Headquarters for the Iowa Department of Transportation was at Ames, so Steve Paulson made an appointment to see Randy Neace, who was Director of Land Operations. "I own 1,120 acres of farm land in Hennepin County," explained Paulson. "My plan is to transform that farm land into a theme park. Before I can do that, however, I need to obtain your cooperation in truncating some of the gravel roads."

"What you want is to have the roads discontinued and barricaded?" asked Neace, seeking clarification of the request.

"That's right. I don't want traffic running across roads that I will convert to my project."

"You know, Mr. Paulson, it isn't just a simple matter of abandoning a road. State law in Iowa requires that certain steps be followed. The main requirement is that at least sixty days prior to any action leading to road abandonment or removal by the Department of Transportation there must be notification by registered mail or personal delivery. The Department sends these letters to all owners of property adjoining the section of road to be abandoned."

"I see. Well, it should simplify the action since I own nearly all the affected land."

"You're right. Nonetheless, we must send the letters. By the way, you will be receiving a letter, too. No doubt there are still a few other property owners who will be impacted—ones who own farm land which border the closed roads. We need to notify all of them about any plans to alter the existing road structure."

"Do you see any problems with the enactment of the road closings, Mr. Neace?"

"I don't think so, providing we get it all coordinated with county and state zoning commissions. Land classification will need to be moved from agricultural use to entertainment use. It also must abide by environmental restrictions."

"Yes, yes. Those items will be taken care of. I'm just interested in your opinion about the road closings. How long do you think it will be until the final consent?"

"Oh, I'd say within three to six months," replied Neace.

"Good. That will be fine." Paulson said his good-bye and went to his car in the parking lot.

When he slid behind the wheel his cell phone rang. It was Reginald Simpson, and he sounded concerned. "We've run into a snag, Steve. I thought you said you had purchased all those farms."

"I have. Sabo's, Stovdahl's, Tesdahl's and Halvorson's. All of them. Eight hundred acres. You bought Arneson's, and that's 320 acres more. What's the problem?"

My realty agent bought the Arneson land, but when he went to the Hennepin County Court House to pick up the deed, he was told that a further title search showed that the property really didn't belong to John Arneson."

"What?" exclaimed Paulson. "But I bought my property and gave my money. How could a title search be done now, after I've already bought it?"

"As you know, a title search establishes a list of who owned the property in the past and whom they sold it to. It might also reflect tax information, easements, conditions of restrictions and so on."

"Don't tell me something I already know," said Paulson with an exasperated tone. "I know what a title search is. I paid money for those farms and now I own them. End of case."

"Not exactly. You have possession of those farms, but you might not have the *right* of possession to them."

"What's the difference?" asked Paulson.

"Here's an example. Let's say that I buy a pen and loan it to you. You now have possession, but you don't have the right of possession. That remains with me, since I was the one who bought it."

Paulson countered the argument by saying, "If we keep with your analogy, then I can buy the pen from you, and then I both possess it and also have the right of possession. Isn't that true? So if I bought the land from someone, then I would possess it, plus I'd have the right of possession."

Simpson replied by saying, "But here's the complication. What if I didn't actually own the pen that I sold to you? Then you wouldn't legally be the owner."

"I still don't see how that's possible with land that I bought. I have the deeds."

"However, Steve, you have a deed for property that wasn't fully searched. Furthermore, it appears that the other farms weren't properly searched either. You might not own any of the 1,120 acres you thought you did."

"Ridiculous! Who's told you all of this?"

"As I said, my agent found this out from a court house clerk at Holly Springs. Somebody had sent her a letter objecting to the sale of the five farms. The letter referred to a legal challenge he was making to the sale and expressed confidence that the real owners would be revealed. If so, all of our transactions might be reversed and we'd have to turn back the property to the actual owners."

"Who is this person who wrote the letter?" demanded Paulson.

"The clerk couldn't reveal the name to me, but it's quite clear that the property, since the deeds are being challenged, belongs to nobody, and that nobody includes you."

"What are we going to do?" Paulson wailed.

"My guess is that before too long you'll get a letter from the individual who's contesting all this. He might want to make you some kind of an offer, hoping that you'll pay him to drop his objections."

Reginald Simpson's prediction proved partially true, for Paulson received a letter, with a return address of Anders Vickdahl. No doubt the writer had found Paulson's address in Des Moines through a simple Google search.

> Dear Mr. Paulson:
>
> I understand that you intended to purchase five farms in Hennepin County. I don't know for sure what your plans are for this farm land, but I need to inform you that the property is not salable. The previous owners might have lived on the land and thought they could sell it, but that was not the case. The land was not theirs to sell, which means that you don't own it now. I have initiated legal action to return the land to the rightful owner. At the conclusion of the proceedings, you will be refunded whatever money you spent.

Vickdahl ended the letter by including his address, e-mail and telephone number. Paulson quickly called the number and found that Vickdahl was at home. He wasted no time getting to the point.

"What do you mean by obstructing the purchase of my land?" Mr. Vickdahl.

"But it isn't yours, Mr. Paulson. I told you that in the letter."

"Who do you think owns it then?" Paulson replied angrily.

"I can't tell you that right now, but you'll find out in due time."

"Do you think that you own it?"

"There's a good chance that I might own some of it, but I really can't say any more."

This pronouncement grated Paulson and he firmly intended to meet Vickdahl and put an end to the irritation.

Chapter 15

✷ ✷ ✷

The Meeting [1855]

In the next few weeks Otto got to know his Norwegian neighbors, buying a cow from Torin Halvorson. He also made a trip to Fort Des Moines to obtain the deed for the 160 acres of land. Before he left, he told Sigurd Helland, "If you still have that blue and white currency, that seems to be worthless around here, I can take it with me and redeem it for you at Fort Des Moines."

"Wonderful," said Sigurd excitedly. "Even if they won't give you a dollar for it, take whatever they offer, for I've always said that 'crumbs are also bread.'"

While in Fort Des Moines, Otto decided to stop by the District Land Office to see the Chief Clerk, Isaac Cooper, who had been so helpful to him earlier in the summer. Cooper had been the person who had suggested that Otto travel to northern Iowa to look for land.

"Well, well, if it isn't Otto Arneson," said Cooper, as he stood up from behind his desk and warmly shook Otto's hand.

"I wasn't sure you would remember me, Mr. Cooper, for I'm certain you meet many people each day."

"Oh, but you're special. Since you saved Frank Allen's life, he stops by frequently to see if I've had any word from you. Actually, I'm surprised you haven't visited before now."

"Why is that?" asked Otto.

"Because you were looking for land, and I told you it would be important to fill out an application at our office once you staked a claim to the land you intended to buy."

Otto put his hand to his forehead. "I completely forgot about that, Mr. Cooper. Yes, you did tell me that. I guess that I've been so busy getting settled on the property that it slipped my mind."

"Did you find land?"

"Yes, up by Eldora in Barren County."

"Come over to our plat map and show me."

Once Otto saw the Iowa River, it was easy to find his land. "Here it is. Oh, and there's the eighty acres I bought from Egil Larson. His farm borders mine, and we both touch the river. I have the deed for what used to be his land."

"All right, I'll fill out the application now." Cooper listed the coordinates of Otto's 160. "Can you pay me the $200 for the land now?"

"Yes, I brought the money with me, since I was expecting to get the deed today."

"No, Mr. Arneson. Like I said back in June, the application is sent to Washington, DC. They will then send back a patent deed for you to pick up. It will take time for all of this, probably two or three months. You'll need to come back in November to pick up the deed."

Otto was disappointed, for that meant another trip from Barren County to Polk County. Hopefully the weather would be all right that time of the fall so that it would be a pleasant trip. The thought crossed his mind that maybe Isaac Cooper, as Chief Clerk, might be able to give him some insight on the ideas he was going to present to his fellow Norwegians.

"Mr. Cooper, would you have a few minutes to answer some questions I have regarding land ownership?"

"All right. I can do that. What do you want to know?"

"There are five of us Norwegian families who live as neighbors in

Barren County. They all have deeds for the land they own. All together, we have over 1,000 acres. The five of us regard land ownership very highly. What we would like to do is to pass our land down from generation to generation. We don't want to lose our property, but want it to stay in our families. My thought is that the five of us need to somehow band together and form an agency which would protect our ownership of the land. This agency would continue throughout the years. When the five of us are dead, the agency would still be there to make sure our children would always have the land. Do you understand what I would like?"

"I believe I do, Mr. Arneson. I think what you're talking about is something called a trust. I know some business people in Fort Des Moines who have done this. The people I am familiar with who have created trusts are typically wealthy individuals who want to keep their business holdings rather anonymous. They use a trust to protect their holdings and preserve them for their descendants."

"How do I get one of these trusts created? Can you make one for me?"

Isaac Cooper rolled his head to one side and chuckled. "No, that's not my line of work. You need to see a lawyer to write one up. If you wish, I can recommend a lawyer who might do that."

"I would appreciate that," said the Norwegian immigrant.

Otto took his leave of the Land Office and walked to the address that Isaac Cooper had given him. It was a bank. He entered and asked for Michael Lindley, who it turned out, was Assistant Legal Counsel for the bank. Otto explained his original idea, along with the new information supplied by Isaac Cooper.

"What you want to do, Mr. Arneson, could be done with a land agreement, such as a trust. A land trust has trustees, who hold legal title to all trust property."

"Who could be trustees?" asked Otto, who was trying to understand the terminology. When he heard Lindley say that the trustees would hold the title to the property, it bothered him. He didn't want to surrender the title.

"They could be anybody, but usually an attorney, a banker, even your friends who have some economic wisdom. In addition, the named beneficiaries of the trust retain use of the property and any income it generates."

"I don't understand what you mean when you use the word 'beneficiaries.'"

"A beneficiary is a person who would live on your land after the five of you are dead; and who would continue to operate it and reap its rewards. The beneficiary would take the profits each year from the income generated by crops raised on the land or animals that were kept on the farm."

Lindley adjusted his glasses and continued. "From a privacy standpoint, a trust is superior to business agencies such as corporations. There is generally no requirement to register the trust. Nor are there public records of who the trustees are."

Otto's mind was working to grasp the information. "What do the trustees do?"

"The trustees keep control of the trust records and the identity of the beneficiaries. They also collect money from the beneficiaries for the purpose of paying the taxes on the property." Lindley gave Otto a penetrating look as though he were looking into his mind. "If I were in your position, I would be rather hesitant to turn over property to trustees, not knowing if they might seize the land and take it away from your family, once you are gone."

Otto admitted that he was wondering about this possibility.

"You needn't worry because this trust could be made irrevocable, which means that the trust cannot be changed. I will construct it so that the land can never pass into the personal control of any of the trustees." Then Lindley asked an unusual question. "Are you a vain man, Mr. Arneson?"

"What do you mean?"

"When the five of you create the trust, you will be giving up ownership of the 1,000 acres. You can no longer proudly state that you are actual owners of the land. Would this bother you?"

"I guess it would. I prize land ownership. It's very important for me that I provide a way for my descendants to always have a place to live and to be financially secure from the profits of the land."

A pause lingered, after which Otto asked, "Can you write a trust for us, Mr. Lindley, so that we don't have to give up our deeds?"

"No, because you can't have it both ways. If you want to safeguard your property for the future, you'll need to relinquish your ownership now. However, you must understand that the farmland will always be there to provide income for your descendants."

Otto rose from his chair and paced behind it. This was not exactly the kind of agency he envisioned. It was necessary to make a choice. If he wanted to ensure that the land would afford security to his later generations, then he would be forced to give up his property rights now.

"I must look to the future, Mr. Lindley. I'll do what needs to be done for my children, grandchildren, and great-grandchildren. Go ahead and write up the trust."

"Very well, but I'll need to know who you want as your trustees."

"How about you? said Otto."

"Fine. In fact, I was going to suggest that there be two or three officers from the bank. I think that we should also have somebody from the county where you live; that's Barren County. We could place one of the lawyers from the county seat, Boulder City, on the board of trustees."

"There is one other person I'd like to have as a trustee," Otto said.

"Who?"

"Mr. Frank Allen."

"Why, he's the Street Commissioner for Fort Des Moines. How do you know him?"

"Back in June my family and I first came to the city and I just happened to be in the right place at the right time to help him out. He had fallen into the Des Moines River and we pulled him to safety."

"I'm impressed. Certainly we can include him. I'll contact him to see if he would serve. In the meantime, you need to locate a lawyer in Boulder City to serve as a trustee."

"There's one last question I have," said Otto. He pulled out the blue and white bill that Sigurd had given him. "A friend of mine had received this the last time he was in Fort Des Moines, but he says that merchants in Eldora won't accept it as currency. Can you redeem this for me and give me a dollar's worth of gold coin for it?"

Lindley took the bill and examined it with interest. "I'm not sure.

Please wait here and I'll be right back." He returned with the bill and said, "The bill is not worth a dollar."

"I was expecting something like that, Mr. Lindley. How much can you offer?"

"I could go as high as ten dollars for it."

"Ten dollars!" coughed Otto. "But it says just one dollar on the front."

"Yes, but this was issued by our bank by mistake. See the how the woman and the cow are off to the left side of the bill? They should have been in the middle. The printer made a mistake on ten of these and left the front with this wide empty border on the right side."

"And that makes it more valuable?" asked Otto.

"It certainly does, to a collector such as I. I have one of the ten bills already. This makes a second if you will sell it to me."

"I sure will," Otto readily agreed. Sigurd would be elated with the news.

It was decided that Otto and the other Norwegians would come to Fort Des Moines in November to sign the trust agreement, the same time that Otto could pick up the deed for his property from the Land Office.

Before Otto left the city, he visited Frank Allen, who was elated to see this brave immigrant who had plucked him from the river. Allen listened to Otto's plan to set up a trust, agreeing to be one of the trustees. He also assured Otto about the integrity of Michael Lindley and the bank. Otto returned to Barren County and relayed to his four Norwegian friends what he had found out from his visit to Des Moines. All of them expressed the same misgivings that Otto had about surrendering their personal ownership to their lands. After an anguished discussion, they concurred that the land trust was an acceptable idea, for they all wanted to have their descendants secured with benefits from the farms.

The first part of October was a happy time for these neighbors. Sigurd Helland's wife and children arrived. As a special present, he used some of the money Otto received for the rare bill and bought a couple of nice warm blankets that would be used on the two beds for his newly arrived wife and children.

The four men left for Fort Des Moines the first part of November. Otto visited the land office and obtained his deed from Isaac Cooper. The men then took their deeds to the bank and signed the papers to create the Friends of Norway Trust. As they read over the document, Mr. Lindley told them, "I added one point here, gentlemen." He used plain words to clarify this last item of the trust. "Do any of you object to it?"

The five men had a brief conversation, and then Otto spoke for the group. "I'm not sure why we need it, but since it appears it won't bring any harm to us five, our children nor our grandchildren, we have no objection." As it would turn out, this provision would be a significant factor 156 years later.

Chapter 16

✳ ✳ ✳

Anders Vickdahl [Iowa 2011]

Steve Paulson looked at a man who resembled many of the other men he had met lately in Hennepin County. This man appeared to be from Scandinavian descent: sandy haired, but infused with a dusting of grey. Wire-framed spectacles surrounded his soft blue eyes.

"Mr. Paulson?" asked Anders Vickdahl, as he opened his front door.

"That's right," returned Paulson.

"Please come in."

Once they were seated in Vickdahl's Des Moines home, Paulson got right to the point. "Your interference has the potential for causing me a lot of problems. You already know that I have purchased over 1,000 acres. What you're doing is like sticking an iron bar in a moving wheel. It would ruin everything I have put in motion."

Vickdahl was unruffled by the announcement. "What are you planning to use the land for, Mr. Paulson?"

"I don't have to give you the details, but I will tell you that it involves a huge entertainment project."

"No doubt it will make you a rich man, Mr. Paulson. For you, the land is merely a business venture, but it's something entirely different for me. You see, I believe I might be a legal owner of the 1,000 acres."

"You mentioned that in our telephone conversation. How is that possible?"

Vickdahl revealed some of the information Paulson was unaware of, "I'm descended from one of the original owners."

"You mean one of the Norwegian ancestors?"

"That's right. I'd like to tell you about one of them, Otto Arneson, who came here from Norway in 1855."

"How do you know so much about him?" taunted Paulson.

Vickdahl calmly replied, "I've taken a deep interest in genealogy and have done a lot of work to find out about my Norwegian ancestors."

"If you know so much about them, fill me in, so I can decide if you're just blowing hot air with your claim to know all about your ancestry."

"As I said, Arneson came here in 1855 with a wife and two children. He quickly bought eighty acres and then 160 acres more. He and four of his Norwegian neighbors formed an alliance to preserve all of their land, which totaled 1,120 acres."

"What do you mean, an alliance?"

"Arneson was a forward thinking man. He got his neighbors to join him in creating a trust, the purpose of which was to keep the land in their possession, and in the possession of their descendants." For the benefit of Paulson, Anders enlarged upon how the trust was set up and a few of its provisions.

"However," continued Anders, "Otto eventually had misgivings about the trust and whether it would be able to fulfill the original intent. He thought that it might be better if he could somehow reduce the consequences of his neighbors' possible whims and changes of thought. Thus, he set about buying their farms over a fifteen-year period."

"Now, how would you know this?" asked Paulson.

"As I said, I've spent a lot of time with genealogy over the years. I've gathered a huge amount of information by reading old letters, diaries and correspondence. Then there are old newspaper clippings and other documents which are readily available public records. I've also listened to a lot of stories handed down by my ancestors."

Paulson wasn't quite sure if he should believe Vickdahl, so he said, "Give me some examples,"

"The first person he bought out was Jacob Anderson, whose property was hampered by not being on a source of water. Sigurd Helland was the next person to sell. Helland had been one of Arneson's first friends, by the way, so it was easy to sell to a friend. After that, Per Bremse turned over his land to Otto. What made it acceptable for all three of these to sell their property was that Otto told them they could stay right on the land. They wouldn't have to move. In fact, their children would be able to live there, too, once the three men passed on. In a way, you might say they were renting the land, with the advantage that they didn't have to pay any rent."

"Is that all of the original owners?"

"No," said Vickdahl. "There was Torun Halvorson. He owned the largest parcel—320 acres. Otto had approached Torun many times, but Halvorson had always refused. Then in 1880 Halvorson was badly injured in a farm accident. He was trying to untangle some corn stocks out of his plowshare when the team of horses pulling the plow spooked and ran over Torun. He lingered for months before he died. During his ill health, he admitted to Otto that his only son, Bjorn, was a spendthrift and would probably not be able to keep the farm if he inherited it. Bjorn was always making bad economic decisions and going into debt. Torun decided it would be better for his wife and four daughters if he could sell the land now and prevent Bjorn from losing it."

"You sound pretty convincing so far," said Paulson. "Tell me more."

"I'll have to go back about 170 years. Otto had a wife named Andrine. Back in Norway before the two were married, she and another man, called Casper Hermundson Tveit, had a son out of wedlock. The child was placed in an orphanage since Andrine could not marry the man. Casper couldn't bear to have the boy in the orphanage, so he took him out. Andrine never knew this until later. Well, a couple of years later Andrine married Otto Arneson, and they came to America. Otto never knew about the child. Casper really loved Andrine, so he followed them to Iowa, bringing the little boy. Casper changed his name to Kasberg Hermansen

Vickdahl, named his infant son Peder and established a home in Fort Des Moines. He never got married. I guess he was only going to love one woman during his lifetime, and that was Andrine. Peder Vickdahl was my greatgreatgrandfather." Anders stopped talking and looked at Paulson.

Astounded with the narrative, Paulson cleared his throat and said, "That doesn't insert you into Arneson's lineage. Maybe this lady named Andrine's, but not Otto Arneson's. You haven't said anything to substantiate having Arneson blood running in you."

"I don't claim to. Peder Vickdahl married one of the daughters of Per Bremse. I'm descended from that Norwegian family. If the trust can be found to still be valid, then all the descendants of those five Norwegian families retain rights to the land, and I'm one of them."

"Let's get back to that trust," said Paulson. "It appears to me that Otto Arneson couldn't legally buy the land of his four neighbors, because that would violate the provisions of the trust."

"It seemed that way to me, too," agreed Vickdahl. "Otto moved the trust headquarters from Fort Des Moines to the county seat shortly after 1855. He got one of the local lawyers to oversee the trust. The people in Fort Des Moines just sort of melted out of the picture. The local lawyer, I guess, was rather remiss and didn't bother to enforce the provisions of the trust. Those things happen. Because of the neglect by the local trustees, Otto started buying his neighbors land. I'm sure he wasn't trying to undermine the arrangement. More likely, he just felt that owning all the land by himself would be a more dependable way to keep it all in control."

"Now here's an interesting piece of history." Paulson leaned forward in his chair, obviously fascinated with the story Vickdahl was unfolding. "In 1855 the five Norwegians lived in Barren County, and Boulder City was the county seat. However, Iowa grew during the next five years, resulting in some of the original counties in the state being reformed. In 1860 Barren County was dissolved and merged into another county—Hennepin County. Boulder City ceased as a county seat, replaced with Holly Springs, miles away. With the discontinuance of the old county and the formation of the new county, many records were lost, misplaced or discarded."

"Let's get back to that trust," interrupted Paulson. "Where are the copies of the trust?"

"That's my point. Because of what I just said—counties merging, passage of time, neglect and so on—apparently there aren't any left," said Vickdahl.

"Are you saying that the copies of the trust don't exit anymore?" inquired Paulson.

"They might, or they might not. Personally, I think they do, for the information handed down by my relatives suggests that Otto was a very cautious person and wanted to make sure that somebody could find the trust. Speculation is that he hid a copy."

"Do you know where it's hidden?" asked Paulson.

"No, I haven't found it, but Otto left clues about the location."

Paulson said, "If the land was to be kept in trust, then nobody owns it now. You can't own it. It's still owned by the trust."

"Nobody knows the answer to that until we find the trust and the will," said Vickdahl.

Paulson jerked his head around when he heard this new wrinkle. "You mentioned a will. What does that have to do with the trust?"

"The story I've been told is that Otto made a will before he died, claiming to alter the provisions of the trust, which was an irrevocable trust. You see, by the time he died in 1885, he was the sole owner of all the land. The other Norwegians had sold their land to him, so he became the single principal involved in the trust. It's possible the trust is still valid today, but we'll never know until we find both it and the will."

"Let me play along with your story, Vickdahl. You say the original document provided for the trust collecting income and paying expenses. And you said that the arrangements of the trust might have been changed over the years. Didn't any of the Norwegian people on the land ever wonder why they weren't being asked by the trustees for money for the purpose of paying taxes to the county, state and federal government?"

"Good point. Quite obviously the people who lived on these farms in recent years paid their own taxes directly. However, remember that over the course of 156 years, county officials die, lawyers die, banks go out of business, records get misplaced. People forget quite innocently what is supposed to be done."

Paulson just sat in his chair, hands on his knees, trying to comprehend all that he had been told. "I've never heard such a story," he finally said. "What do you propose we do now?"

"There's nothing you can do, except wait. As for me, I intend to find the trust and the will. Once they're found, I'm sure that will reveal the proper status of the land."

Chapter 17

* * *

The Hunt (Iowa 2011)

After Paulson left Vickdahl's house, Anders sat down at his desk and took out a sheet of paper to begin listing what he knew that might help him find the hidden trust and will. He was a fairly successful author, having published dozens of mystery books. Putting ideas down on paper is exactly what the main character of his books did in order to sift through and make sense of all the facts. He made a good living from the royalties of his books; therefore, he had enough time to be flexible in how he organized his days. Anders didn't have to punch a time clock or work in somebody's company, which meant he could choose his own hours for the investigation.

I don't know:

1. Where is the trust document?
2. Where is Otto's will?
3. What are the clues to help me find the hidden trust and will?
4. Where are the clues?

I know:

1. A trust had been set up for the five Norwegians
2. Otto had bought all the farms, so he ended up owning 1,120 acres
3. Modern Hennepin County covers the area of old Barren County
4. It seems Otto wanted somebody, later, to be able to find the trust document and the will
5. It seems Otto probably wanted it to be found by a person he would feel very fond of or close to, or would be located in a place that had connections to someone he was close to
6. Steve Paulson has no information which would be of help in finding the hidden trust and will

The length of the two lists indicated he knew more than what he didn't know, but that didn't make discovery of the hidden location any more certain. How should he go about his search? Anders decided that it would be necessary to drive to Hennepin County and visit the cemetery where Otto Arneson was buried. He made the 165-mile drive in two and a half hours. The old Fjelvik Cemetery was located across the road from the church that Otto and his Norwegian neighbors had attended. The original church had been made of wood and had burned down back in the mid 1900s, and had been rebuilt as a brick structure. Anders ambled through the cemetery. He had visited it before to look at the grave markers of his Bremse relatives, but had never looked for Otto Arneson's. The ones erected in recent decades, he observed, were granite, most rose colored or grey. Older ones were carved from a variety of rock: sandstone, limestone and marble. Anders found Otto's grave, marked by an eight-foot obelisk. The front side had his name with the dates of 1825-1885. What looked like a small stone bucket had been sculpted to the top, as a finial. Of course the bucket was solid; it had no opening, so it wouldn't collect rainwater. Anders walked around the obelisk. On the back side was an inscription, in Norwegian, quite faded from decades of weathering. He carefully copied the words and, knowing some Norwegian, translated the lines:

"Look at the memory of Andrine.
Find her tine."

What did that mean? Of course, Andrine was Otto's wife. What was the meaning of "Look at the memory"? Also, what is a tine?

He drove into Holly Springs and went to the library, where he hoped to find a Norwegian-English dictionary. If not, he could use his laptop computer and google "tine." The dictionary he found defined it as a round wooden container used in Norway. He also found a picture of one on the Internet. It didn't look very large. Now that he thought of it, the carved finial on top of Otto's monument looked similar to the Internet photo on his laptop. The inscription directions said to find Andrine's tine, but where would it be?

Deciding to return to Fjelvik Cemetery, Anders looked again at Otto's monument. There was nothing he hadn't seen before. But the first line of the inscription said to look at the memory of Andrine. He examined Andrine's gravestone, beside Otto's. It wasn't a tall monument like her husband's. Rather, hers was simply a headstone, about three feet high. Hers, too, bore an inscription:

"My tine holds all that was precious
And all that is precious.
Dig behind my name
To find the tine."

"Dig behind my name." That might mean that there was something buried behind her headstone. There was only one way to find out. He hurried back to his car and drove to K-Mart to buy a shovel and a pair of gloves. Returning to the cemetery, he dug into the rich black loam Iowa soil. About a foot below the sod, he struck some wood. It broke into pieces. Another thrust with the shovel and he struck metal. Lifting the wooden pieces, he saw that it had once been a round basket—a tine. Inside was a metal box. He opened it and found papers: Otto's will, Kasberg's original letter to Andrine, along with more letters sent back and forth between Andrine and her son, Peder. The trust was also there. Anders read over the trust. It seemed that a bank lawyer from Fort Des Moines named Michael Lindley had inserted a point in the trust back in 1855:

> "If any of the descendants of any of the original Norwegian owners move off the land, then they forfeit their right to benefit from the trust. Their part of the 1,120 acres becomes property of the state of Iowa, to be preserved as a piece of Norway, populated with flowers, trees and plants from Norway, left in a state of nature so it can look like the "old country."

The implications of the trust clearly signified that the 1,120 acres now belonged to the state of Iowa. None of the descendants of the five Norwegians now lived on the farmland. Anders never was a direct descendant, so he was excluded from any benefits of the trust. Anders' twenty-five-year-old son had never lived on the property, much less owned any of it.

The will that Otto had made was a simple one. Since Andrine had died a year before Otto, he had bestowed all of his property and many of his possessions to his son, Nils. And he had willed a significant amount of money to his daughter, Sigrid. There was nothing in the way of secret bequests to friends or neighbors. However, folded up inside the will were several sheets of paper, handwritten by Otto. When Anders read them, he realized they were disclosures about events that concerned Otto's wife.

I expect these papers will be read by somebody long after I am dead. They do not present a confession, for the events are long past confessing. I am simply trying to clear up events that happened long ago.

Before Andrine and I were married, she had a child with another man; but she never married him. The child was put in an orphanage. When Andrine and I—and our own two children—left Norway, she thought she would never see the man, who came to be known as Kasberg Vickdahl and the child. Unknown to Andrine and me, Kasberg withdrew the child, whom he named Peder, from an orphanage in Norway and followed us to America. The two of them lived in Fort Des Moines.

In 1864 Kasberg Vickdahl revealed to Peder the identity of his real mother. Up until this time Kasberg had misled Peder, making up a lie that Kasberg's wife (Peder's mother) had died back in Norway. Kasberg told him the truth, which was that his real mother was in the United States living right here in Iowa. Peder demanded to know who she was. Kasberg didn't think that was possible, for doing so would result in me knowing the story, too. Kasberg agonized over the predicament, for he was concerned for my well being. He believed that such a revelation would be a terrible thing for me to learn.

That same year of 1864 Kasberg wrote a letter to Andrine, explaining all that had happened and that he and Peder were living in Fort Des Moines. Peder wanted to meet Andrine. Andrine wrote back to Kasberg and said that I already knew about her past. She had kept the secret too long and wanted to unburden herself to her husband. She told me that she felt love and affection for me, and not Kasberg. But she would like to see the son she had abandoned in Norway. Andrine and I traveled to Fort Des Moines to meet Kasberg and Peder. There was a tearful reunion between Andrine and the son she had not seen since he was just a few days old.

Andrine and I never saw Kasberg again. We never told our Norwegian neighbors in Hennepin County about this part of Andrine's life. Peder later moved to Hennepin County, where he became a lawyer. He fell in love with one of Per Bremse's daughters (Berta) and married her in 1877. He was 34 and she was 20.

If the person who finds this is a stranger and does not know who I am, then the story will be empty and meaningless.

*If the person is somebody who does know who I am, then the
story will possibly clear up questions from history.*

Signed: Otto Arneson   *Dated: June 6, 1885*

Vickdahl returned to Des Moines with all of the documents he had
unearthed. He decided to call Paulson right away to set up a meeting so
that the man could see how the trust would impact any hopes he had of
keeping the land he thought he had purchased.

Paulson eagerly accepted his invitation and showed up at Vickdahl's
house at the arranged time. "Let me take your coat," offered Anders.

"No, that's all right. I'll just keep it on."

Anders showed the metal box he had unearthed, took out the
documents, and placed them on the table. He first read the will to show that
it contained nothing which would be of any significance to the situation.

"Now this document has a great deal of importance to you. Much
more to you than to me." He read the trust, pausing before he recited the
item that Lindley had added at the end.

When he had completed reading the trust, Anders put it down. Paulson,
through tightened lips, said, "I want to look at it myself." He grabbed the
paper and after a few minutes, slammed it down on the table.

The act made Vickdahl blink several times.

"This trust document would certainly foil all that I have done so far."
Then he added slowly, "If anybody ever saw it, that is."

"Of course they'll see it. It's a legal document. I plan to take it to an
attorney and have that verified," responded Anders.

"No, I don't think that will happen. I'm too deep into this to let this
document be made public."

"What do you mean when you said you were too deep into this? Is it
because you've invested too much money? You can get the money back
when the land sales are repealed."

"Oh, it's more than that." Paulson's eyes took on a gleam which revealed
a streak of conceit and arrogance. "I've done a good many things in order
to acquire all those farms."

Vickdahl was unnerved with Paulson's words. "What have you done?"

Paulson couldn't help but continue since he had to boast to somebody. "Do you think I bought all those farms because the land just happened to become available? That's ridiculous. I planned them all." With increasing intensity, he explained what he had done to poison Elmer Sabo, how he had shot Milo Tesdahl and Ronald Stovdahl and how he had driven Arnold Halvorson and John Arneson off.

"You can't be telling the truth, Paulson. Only some monster would do all those things."

"You're wrong there. Only a brilliant person could ever accomplish them," crowed Paulson. Then he reached into his coat and pulled out a revolver. "I don't want you to get in my way, so I'm afraid that the only solution is to eliminate you."

Anders rose slowly from his chair and moved to his left so that Paulson had his back to the hallway. "Wait, Paulson, don't shoot me. There's something else you should know."

"Oh, yeah! What is that?"

As Paulson uttered the final word, a voice behind him said, "This is the police, Paulson, put your gun away." The hard barrel of the Glock pistol pushed into Paulson's back. Paulson turned to see two police officers. He slowly lowered his own gun and one of the officers removed it from his hand.

It was though a beach ball had been deflated. Where Paulson was filled with his self-importance just a few seconds earlier, now he was slumped, with head bent.

"Thank you, Mr. Vickdahl, for your part in this. You were correct when you thought that Paulson would make some threats when he was given the information. When you came to us with your concerns, you did the right thing. Our plan to conceal ourselves in the bedroom worked well, right up to the point where you maneuvered yourself so that he had his back to the hallway. We didn't realize, though, that he would make a confession to all those crimes." One of the officers read Paulson his Miranda rights, placed him in handcuffs and took him off to jail.

When they had all left, Anders went to the sofa and sat down heavily.

He exhaled a loud burst of air, lifted his head to the ceiling and closed his eyes. He gave a few words of prayerful thanks for escaping any harm. Then he thought of the 1,120 acres of land. It would not be a theme park, run for the profit of the detestable Steve Paulson. Instead, it would be a tranquil preserve of Norwegian trees, flowers and plants. A piece of Otto Arneson's Norway in the middle of Iowa.

Glossary

* * *

Meanings of Selected Norwegian Words

Bare bra, takk: Fine, thank you.

Far: father

Fylke: an administrative unit in Norway, similar to a county

God dag: good afternoon

Husman: a person who farms other people's land, and simply rents the house

Hvordan står det til?: How are you?

Min sønn: my son

Selvier: a farmer in Norway who owns his own land

Tine: a small round wooden basket with a lid